SEXY motherpucker

A Bad Motherpuckers Novel

By Lili Valente

SEXY motherpucker

By Lili Valente

―――――――――――

Self Taught Ninja Press

Copyright © 2017 Lili Valente
All rights reserved
ISBN 13: 978-1546343813

All Rights Reserved
Copyright **Sexy Motherpucker** © 2017 Lili Valente

All rights reserved. Without limiting the rights under copyright reserved above, no part of this publication may be reproduced, stored in or introduced into a retrieval system, or transmitted, in any form, or by any means (electronic, mechanical, photocopying, recording, or otherwise) without the prior written permission of the copyright owner. This erotic romance is a work of fiction. Names, characters, places, brands, media, and incidents are either the product of the author's imagination or are used fictitiously. The author acknowledges the trademarked status and trademark owners of various products referenced in this work of fiction, which have been used without permission. The publication/use of these trademarks is not authorized, associated with, or sponsored by the trademark owners. This book is licensed for your personal use only. This book may not be re-sold or given away to other people. If you would like to share this book with another person, please purchase an additional copy for each person you share it with, especially if you enjoy hot, sexy, emotional romantic comedies featuring alpha males. If you are reading this book and did not purchase it, or it was not purchased for your use only, then you should return it and purchase your own copy. Thank you for respecting the author's work.

Cover design by Bootstrap Designs. Editorial services provided by Help Me Edit.

About the Book

When the family dog trots in with my diaphragm in its mouth—in front of my date, his parents, and his adorable little girl—you would think I'd hit rock bottom.

WRONG.

Let's back this up a sec…

Brendan Daniels is the sexiest man alive. The captain of the Badger's NHL team is also clever, kind, funny, and was my good friend…until we cruised out of the friend zone one weekend with a red-hot fling. Come Monday morning, I wanted to keep riding the Big O train to happy town, but Brendan wanted someone who was "stepmom" material.

A.K.A, not me, apparently.

The problem? I'm crazy in love with him and his daughter. So when he asks me to be his pretend girlfriend for a long weekend with his former in-laws, I say yes. We're still friends, after all, and friends don't let friends fake it alone.

***

Laura Collins is the last woman I should be thinking about taking in the back seat of my car, in the woods behind my in-laws' house, or in a hotel room where we're sharing one very small, very squeaky bed.

I need a steady, stable influence for my daughter, not a fling with this too wild, too young, too impulsive red head. So what if she's beautiful and intense and passionate and has the biggest heart I've ever known?

I don't want to fall in love. I really don't. The whole "pretend girlfriend" thing was supposed to solve my problems, buy me a little more time.

But when it comes to Laura?

Hell, maybe I'm just not cut out for faking it.

Dedicated to Sawyer Bennett, one generous, kind, talented, kick-ass writer friend. Glad to know you, lady.

SEXY MOTHERPUCKER

PROLOGUE

Laura
Last summer...

The summer breeze off the Pacific is cool and sweet, and the setting sun casts a sleepy orange glow over Cannon Beach. Majestic Haystack Rock rises from the waves a few hundred feet from shore, a benevolent overlord gazing on as families take advantage of the shortest night of the year to party long after most of these kids would usually be in bed asleep.

All in all, it's an excellent evening for burning underwear.

"Good-bye silk thong," I say, tossing my favorite, most comfortable thong onto the fire. It catches on one of the unburned driftwood limbs, trembling there as if hoping for a last-minute rescue from the flames licking upward.

But there will be no rescue. All the underthings must go. I've got the entire contents of my lingerie drawer in the duffle bag slung over my shoulder, and I'm not leaving until every bra, panty, and garter belt has been reduced to ashes.

"Good-bye, comfortable cotton briefs." I drop a handful of simple black and white briefs into the heart of the fire, where they begin to smolder. "Good-bye lace boy-shorts. Good-bye push-up bra, I knew you well."

A soft rumble of laughter alerts me to the fact I'm not alone.

I spin, eyes narrowed, to see Brendan standing behind me in a white button-up with sleeves rolled to the elbow, khaki shorts, and bare feet, looking ridiculously gorgeous, as usual. The man should come with a warning label—Danger: Do Not Look Directly into These Dreamy Blue Eyes for Too Long or You Will Forget That I am Off-Limits, Not Interested in Romance, and Also Irritating as Fucking Hell.

Brendan is captain of the Portland Badgers, the NHL team my PR efforts have helped lift from relative obscurity to become one of the big names in the league. The fact that they've qualified for the playoffs three out of the past five years probably hasn't hurt, but I'm not afraid to take credit where credit is due. I've grown the Badger youth hockey program, increased season-ticket sales by twenty percent, and started a fantasy camp with a waiting list two hundred people deep.

I work hard for my team, and I appreciate players who make my job easy by being sweet to reporters, putting their best skate forward when I film spots to play during the games, and smiling for the camera at meet-and-greets designed to build goodwill within the community.

Brendan is *not* one of those players. Brendan is a cranky, recalcitrant, stand-offish, doesn't-play-well-with-the-press pain in my ass, which makes the big smile on his face even more disconcerting.

Damn, he's nice to look at.

It really is too bad that he's determined to stay above the dating fray. He would make some lucky woman very happy. And maybe make himself easier to live with in the process.

"Sorry to interrupt, but I couldn't help myself." He ambles closer, slipping his hands into his pockets. "I had to see if you were really burning your bra."

"I am. And my panties." I flick another pair of briefs into the flames.

"Is this a feminist thing?" He comes to stand beside me, sending the smell of freshly washed man and an earthy, foresty cologne drifting to my nose.

He must have already been back to his room at the hotel to shower. I'm still in the bikini and oversize cover-up I've been wearing all day, rocking the casual look for the first annual Badger Beach Bum weekend. I'd planned to head up the hill half an hour ago and get cleaned up for the team cocktail party starting at ten, but after a chat with some teenagers who agreed to let me take over maintenance of their beach fire, I decided it was better to burn the underwear first.

The sooner I can put the Panty-gate disaster behind me, the better.

"No, it's not a feminist thing." I wait for the briefs to start smoking before I add more fuel to the fire. "It's a walked in and caught my boyfriend wearing my underwear kind of thing."

Brendan's brows lift sharply. "Oh. Wow."

"Yeah. I forgot my beach bag this morning. When I ran back to get it, I found Henry standing in the middle of my bedroom wearing my lace thong, silk stockings, and push up bra. There was also makeup involved, but that wasn't mine." I toss another bra, proud of how much better my aim is getting. "He's a winter, not a spring."

"I'm guessing this wasn't something you knew about Henry going into the relationship."

"No, it wasn't. Henry is a seemingly straight-laced investment banker whose hobbies include making money, drinking scotch, playing fantasy football, power lifting, and going on long, aggressively competitive bike rides with other investment bankers. He never made any mention of a love for cross-dressing."

"And if he had?" Brendan asks, collecting a slim piece of wood from the sand.

I shake my head. "I don't know. To be honest,

it would probably have still been a deal breaker, but if he'd been upfront about it—and bought his own lingerie instead of tainting mine—it would have at least been up for discussion."

"Wouldn't washing everything work just as well?"

"No, Brendan, washing everything won't work just as well." The next few bras hit the fire with considerably more force. "Some taints go too deep for soap. Some taints must be cleansed by fire."

"Like taints that come from being close to your ex's taint," he says, summoning an unexpected laugh from between my lips.

"Yes, like that." I peek at him from the corner of my eye. "I'm not used to you being funny."

"It's something I try to avoid as much as possible," he says pleasantly. "It confuses people. Makes them think I'm not going to be a pain in their ass the next time they ask me to spend my Sunday morning eating pancakes with strangers."

"So you saw the email…" I glance up at him, my throat tightening for reasons I can't explain.

He nods. "I did."

"There are worse things than being asked to eat pancakes, Brendan."

"Pancakes with strangers," he corrects, using the end of his stick to catch the thong that has thus far escaped the flames. "I don't like strangers."

"Even strangers who are also your biggest

fans?" I watch him lower the panties into the fire, my cheeks flushing for reasons I also can't explain.

"Even strangers who are fans. When I'm not away for a game, Sundays are for family." The thong slides onto the coals, and Brendan turns to me, an all too familiar stubborn expression firming his features. "You can courtesy-copy Coach Swindle and the team manager on requests all you want, but I won't be bullied by any of you. Chloe's back from her grandparents' house on Tuesday so I won't be eating pancakes with anyone next Sunday, or any Sunday in the foreseeable future."

"You can bring Chloe if you want," I say, naively hoping this might be an easy fix. "I would be happy to watch her while you network."

He crosses his arms at his chest. "No."

I take a deep breath, in and out, fighting a wave of irritation. "Come on, Brendan. You know Chloe and I get along like macaroni and cheese. We could eat pancakes together at the kids' table and then color until you're ready to go. It will be fun."

"No."

"No? Just…no?" My volume rises as I drop my nearly empty duffle onto the sand and spread my fingers wide, palms up, in front of the most frustrating man in the universe. "That's it? No, Laura, I will not allow you to do your job. No, Laura, you will never have my cooperation without a fight. No, Laura, I refuse to compromise no matter how far you bend over backward to make things easy for me."

"That's not—"

"No, Laura," I push on, unable to stop the flood now that I've started, "you are a thorn in my side, and I hate you like I hate fans who bang on the glass, so you might as well give up and resign now because you are the worst part of my day. Every day. Bar none."

His gaze softens, and the stubborn jut fades from his jawline. "I don't hate you. Not even a little bit."

I swallow hard, shocked to find my eyes beginning to sting. "Yeah, well sometimes it feels like it. I'm just trying to do my job, you know."

"And I'm just a single dad trying to be there for my daughter."

I nod, the stinging sensation getting even worse. "I know that. And I respect it so much, I really do. I adore Chloe, and would never want to take quality time with her dad away from her, but can't we find a middle ground?"

Brendan's blue eyes wrinkle at the edges. "Are you crying?"

"No." I sniff hard, fighting to hold back the tears insisting it's time to come parachuting out of my tear ducts. "I never cry."

"That doesn't sound healthy."

My bottom lip trembles. "It's fine. I don't need to cry. It's a waste of time. What does it matter if half the people I work with think I'm annoying and useless? I know I do good things for this team."

"No one thinks you're annoying or useless."

"Yes, they do." I sniff again as Brendan's face begins to shimmer from the stupid tears filling my stupid eyes. "But it's fine. Who cares? And who cares if I have to burn all my underwear because I'm not sure what Henry wore when I was gone? And who cares if the first guy I've given a key to my apartment in years didn't trust me enough to be honest about his lady-panty fetish, and I'm clearly a crappy judge of character who will probably end up married to a serial killer? It's fine, I'm just—"

"Stop it." Brendan cups my face in his hands, drawing me closer. His touch is gentle but assured, commanding, and…interesting in ways I've never been interested in Brendan before.

I suck in a breath and hold it, blinking fast. Brendan has only ever been my friend, and there are times when things between us aren't even really that friendly. But his face is suddenly very close to mine, and his eyes are burning with an intensity that is confusing

When he speaks in a soft, husky voice, my pulse begins to beat faster. "I'm sorry I make things hard on you. I'll try to do better."

My forehead furrows. "You will?"

"I will, and I'm going to prove it. Turn around and close your eyes."

My brows shoot up, but before I can ask why I need to turn around, Brendan says, "Do it, Collins. You can trust me."

It's true. If there's anyone I can trust, it's Brendan. He isn't the easiest person to get along with at times, but he is honorable to the core. He is trustworthy and good and, even in his most stubborn moments, kind.

With a nod, I turn to face the ocean. The crowd has thinned considerably in the last half hour. Now there are only a few couples still lounging on their blankets at the far end of the beach, and a trio of horseback riders trotting toward the trail that leads up to the cliffs overlooking the water and continues to the hotel parking lot.

"Okay, you can turn around," Brendan says after a moment.

I turn, a confused smile curving my lips as I see what he's holding in one hand. "Are those boxers?"

"They are." He nods solemnly.

My smile widens. "How did you get them without taking off your shorts?"

"I didn't." He winks as he steps closer to the flames. "I used to be an Olympic-level streaker back in high school. I can get in and out of a pair of shorts in two seconds flat."

"Impressive." I nod, refusing to be flustered by that wink. "But I'm not sure I understand the point of this removal of underwear, Daniels."

"Because I'm going to burn them in a show of solidarity, to help remove the taint of any bad feelings between us. Give us a fresh start."

"Oh," I whisper, surprised by how nice a fresh start sounds.

But then, that's what this is really about. I'm not burning my bras because Henry might have worn them. I'm burning them because I don't want to be the woman who was too proud to admit that things with her too-perfect-to-be-true boyfriend haven't been perfect for a while. That they have, in fact, been pretty shitty.

I want a fresh start, to head back into the dating rat-race with my eyes open. I want to burn away the bullshit and make a commitment to being honest with myself about what I really want in a partner.

"You ready?" Brendan twirls his boxers in a circle.

I nod, reaching for the last handful of panties in my bag. "Ready."

"On the count of three," he says, holding my gaze. "One, two…"

On three, we both drop our drawers into the bonfire. For a moment, the flames dim, fighting for oxygen, but then they surge back even brighter than they were before, illuminating the smile on Brendan's face.

"You should smile more often," I say, nudging him with my elbow.

He nudges me back. "And you should stop

wearing makeup."

I snort. "No way. I look like a twelve-year-old without eyelashes. Or eyebrows. Or lips, unless I have a sunburn."

"No, you don't," he says softly, "you're beautiful, Freckles."

I usually hate any mention of my smattering of offensive nose dots, but when "freckles" is used in the same sentence as "you're beautiful"…

I shift my gaze slowly to my right and find Brendan watching me with that intense look in his eyes again, making it clear he isn't kidding. "Well, thank you. You're not too bad to look at, either."

He smiles as he shifts closer. "No? Not too bad?"

I shrug. "Nah. I mean, I don't throw up in my mouth anymore when I see you coming down the tunnel all sweaty and gross."

He laughs, his eyes doing this sparkling thing that is completely mesmerizing, holding me in thrall as he brushes my hair over my shoulder. "Well, that's good. I don't like tripping a woman's gag reflex."

"Right." I blush hard, pulling a Libby—my little sister excels at turning bright red at the slightest mention of anything sexual—because I'm thinking about other ways a man could trip a woman's gag reflex.

Yes, I'm thinking about Brendan's cock and my mouth and all the fun they could have together. Sue me! I have a dirty mind; I can't help it. And the fact that I know he's free-balling beneath those khakis certainly isn't helping things.

Brendan clears his throat with a soft laugh. "I didn't mean it like that."

"Likely story."

"I didn't." He's still standing way closer to me than he ever has before, sending "gorgeous male in close proximity" alerts tickling across my skin. "I swear. I've been out of the game too long to be that quick with innuendo. I just meant that I enjoy not making you physically ill."

I nod, torn between the urge to step back—hopefully clearing my head—or to lean in, bracing my hands on Brendan's chest. Touching him is starting to seem like a good idea, a really good idea, though I know for a fact it's not. We work together, we fight as often as we laugh, he has a daughter to consider, and my last breakup is so fresh I'm still sporting road rash.

But damn, he's sexy, and he smells incredible, and the way he's looking at me makes my lungs feel too small and my heart feel too large and my fingertips itch to be buried in his softly curled, dirty-blond hair.

"What are you thinking, Collins?" The husky note in his voice strikes a hard blow to my already weakening resolve.

"I was thinking about your quick change," I confess, as he tips his head closer to mine. "What

SEXY MOTHERPUCKER

if I'd turned around too soon?"

"Then I guess you would have gotten an eyeful," he says, his arm wrapping slowly around my waist. "But better bare than wearing your underwear, right?"

"Yes." My pulse spikes as my breasts flatten against his chest, and my body celebrates how incredibly good it feels to be close to this man. I tip my head back, bringing my lips mere inches from Brendan's as I whisper, "I like that you're proceeding cautiously. Giving me plenty of time to come to my senses."

His nose brushes against mine, and his breath is warm on my lips as he asks, "Are you going to come to your senses?"

"I don't think so. That doesn't sound very interesting."

"And what does sound interesting?" His arm tightens around me. "Maybe something like this?"

Before I can respond, his mouth is on mine, and a relieved, elated, dizzily wonderful *wow* feeling rolls through me with a sharp snap. The snap is like a light flicked on in a dark room, a horn blaring on a silent street, the sudden dump of adrenaline into the bloodstream when you start to step off a curb and a car you didn't see coming rushes past a second before your foot leaves the concrete.

The snap shouts, "Pay attention! Something unexpected and potentially dangerous but also exciting is happening!"

And it is.

Cranky, pain-in-my-butt Brendan is kissing me, and it is the most incredible kiss of my entire life. The sweetest, sexiest, most intense kiss, one that turns my bones to jelly and sets off an electrical storm in my nervous system. His tongue strokes against mine, hungry and demanding, asking for what he needs, and I can't help but wrap my arms around his neck and give it to him.

Because what he needs is me—my touch, my kiss, my body welcoming him in as he allows himself to get close to someone for the first time in so long.

***

Later that night, after we skip the cocktail party to spend a few hours naked and lost in each other in the big bed in Brendan's ocean-view room, he holds me close and confesses that it was his first time since his wife died.

"Three years," I whisper, breath rushing out. "Wow."

"Almost three. Three next month."

I press a kiss to his chest, right above his heart. "I'm sorry. And I'm so sorry you and Chloe lost her." I didn't know his wife Maryanne personally—I didn't start working intimately with team members until after the car accident that killed her and put Chloe in the hospital for nearly a month—but I've heard wonderful things about her, this woman who was taken from her family way too soon.

"Thanks." Brendan hugs me closer, eliminating the sliver of air between his skin and mine. "And thank you for this. I was beginning to think I'd never be with someone again. It just felt so wrong every time I tried. But not tonight. Tonight was…good."

I smile grimly. I have no illusions about this being anything but a physical thing, but a girl likes to hear something better than "good."

But I don't let my bruised ego do the talking. I may have a temper sometimes, but I know when to put petty things aside. This man has just slept with a woman for the first time since his wife's death, and that woman is me. And though I had no idea those were the fraught waters I was wading into when I said yes to coming up to his room, that is reality, and I'm big on reality.

And kindness, especially when people are as vulnerable as Brendan is right now.

So I simply kiss his chest again and say, "It was good for me, too."

"Good enough to let me make you come again, Freckles?" He pulls me on top of him, guiding my legs to either side of his hips.

The second my most intimate places brush against his, lightning strikes all over again, and all I can say is, "Yes."

Yes, as he fists one hand in my hair, holding me captive as he kisses me deep and slow while he moves inside me, shooting my soul full of light and bliss. Yes, as he carries me into the shower and we go again with my legs wrapped tight around his hips and my body pinned between the cool tile and his warm skin. Yes, as we fall asleep later with his arm tight around my waist and his voice soft in my ear, telling me he's so glad I decided to stay.

Yes, as one night turns into two and then three, and we secretly stay at the hotel after the rest of the team has left. Yes, as we laugh and talk and take long walks on the beach and have sex like a meteor is on a collision course with earth and we only have two days left to orgasm.

By the time Monday morning rolls around, I wake up feeling so relaxed, happy, and well-fucked that I'm pretty sure nothing can bring me down.

And then I look up to see Brendan already dressed and tucking his carefully folded dirty clothes into his duffle bag.

"Hey." He smiles the awkward smile of a guy who has decided the fun is over. "I didn't want to wake you. You don't need a ride back to the city, do you?"

"No, I have my car." I try not to be hurt by the relief that flashes across his tense features. We've been together constantly for the past three days. It's perfectly natural that he's ready for some alone time.

"Cool. I have practice in two hours. It's already going to be tight getting there on time."

"Right." I tuck the sheet around my chest as I sit up, leaning back against the headboard. "So, will I see you again? I mean, I know I'll see you but..." My throat tightens as I await his response, because sometime in the past two days I stopped thinking of this as a one-weekend stand and started thinking I would like to keep laughing and talking and being with Brendan, to see where this might lead.

"I don't know," he says after a long, uncomfortable beat, his gaze fixed on the duvet we kicked to the end of the bed last night when the room got too hot. "The past few days have been amazing, Laura. But things are...complicated."

Ouch. Complicated. Which means he isn't interested in making an effort to work through the complications so he can keep fucking me on a regular basis. "Right. I get it."

"You're incredible." He finally makes eye contact, though the regret in his gaze makes me wish he hadn't. "You're beautiful and fun and so insanely sexy. But I'm not a twenty-five-year-old kid anymore. I can't let myself get swept up in something just because I'm having a good time. I need stability, for Chloe and for myself. I'm all she's got. I can't start thinking with my dick and let her down."

I nod and keep nodding for way too long, while a hundred different things race through my brain. The possible responses are various shades of hurt, sad, angry, and offended, but what finally comes out is an only slightly wounded-sounding, "I care about Chloe, you know. And if you kept being the very not annoying person I've been with this weekend, I could care about you, too. It doesn't have to be just sex."

He presses his lips together, and in that endless second between my words and his, I die a little inside. "I'm sorry, Laura, I can't."

Okay, I die a lot.

Because no one has ever made me feel as wonderful—or as terrible—as Brendan Daniels.

He took me to sexy new highs and introduced me to excruciatingly embarrassing new lows. I'm probably lucky that this is the first time a man I wanted more than sex from doesn't want more than sex from me. At least for a little while, until he gets tired of me or we realize we hate each other or I discover him dressed in my underwear.

I'm twenty-seven years old, for God's sake. A killer rejection like this had to happen sooner or later, right?

As Brendan slips out the door, I huddle under the covers, trying to forget I ever made close, intimate friends with Mr. Daniel's lovely, talented cock. I intend to sleep late, lick my wounds, and move on, foolishly thinking that will be the end of the pain.

I have no clue that the situation is so much worse than I've assumed.

***

It takes a couple of weeks to realize that I don't simply miss pouncing Brendan's gorgeous body. I miss the way we talked, the way we laughed, the way he pulled me close in the dark and held me like I was the only thing tethering him to our swiftly spinning planet.

By the time I come to terms with the fact that I'm in love with a man who wants nothing more to do with me, Brendan has moved on.

We're back to acting like friends who occasionally irritate the shit out of each other. Except now, every time he looks at me, I feel simultaneously elated and miserable, and I wish I could rewind time so I would never know how right it feels to sleep in his arms.

So, yeah…

So far that fresh start stuff is working out really fucking well.

CHAPTER One

Brendan
Four months later...

I'm too old for this.

I am too goddamned old to be smuggling a mannequin wearing a hot pink thong-kini in through the back door to the locker room, while my friend Justin motions for me to move faster and Wallace and Saunders giggle like third graders somewhere behind me.

I have bigger things to worry about than whether or not Nowicki's rookie initiation prank is the "dopest shit ever," or if we'll get caught by Coach Swindle, who is even older than I am and has even less patience for the constant, adolescent pranking that has become so deeply engrained in the culture of professional hockey that I doubt I'll ever make it through a season without having mayonnaise smeared on my shoes or a plastic snake hidden in my locker.

My only comfort is that this should be over pretty quickly and then I'll be able to move on to the next unpleasant task on my agenda.

At least that one involves a beautiful woman who isn't made of fiberglass.

But the thought offers no comfort. Yes, Laura is a beautiful woman, and yes, simply being in the same room with her is enough to make my blood rush and my skin prickle with awareness, but we're just friends now. Just friends, even though every time I lay eyes on her, all I can think about is how much I want to kiss her and keep kissing her until she's hot and eager and begging me to take her on her desk.

Or up against the wall in her office. Or—

"He's coming. Maybe a minute behind me," Petrov whispers, jabbing a thumb over his shoulder as he ducks into the locker room from the tunnel.

"Quick, get her in there!" Justin hisses, helping me shove the mannequin into Nowicki's open locker. Jus arranges the arms, while I stuff the legs in among Nowicki's copious collection of moldy-smelling tennis shoes. Justin shuts the door softly and with a final fist-pump of victory, relaxes onto the bench in front of his own locker, an utterly bored expression on his face.

"You're too good at that," I mutter.

"I'm going to take up acting after I retire." His lips quirk before settling back into an indifferent line. "Now scram. Your prank face sucks. Go pack your bag or something."

"My bag's already packed," I grumble as I wander over to the couches on the other side of the room, pretending to watch Sports Center while I replay the script I wrote for myself last night when I realized I had no choice but to ask Laura for help.

I think it's good. Respectful, with some quid pro quo offered to make it clear I'm trying not to be a selfish bastard.

But asking her for a favor like this is still going to be awkward and uncomfortable, whether she says "yes" or "hell no."

Fuck. If she says no, I don't know what I'm going to do…

She has to say yes. I have to convince her, even if I have to grovel on my hands and knees to do it.

I'm dimly aware of the too-loud conversation on the other side of the locker room as Saunders and Wallace do a shitty job of playing it cool, and the rush of the showers someone turned on so it wouldn't be too quiet in here when Nowicki walks in, but somehow I miss the rookie's entrance. When he suddenly screams like someone grabbed his arm and plunged it into the center of a fire pit, I flinch hard enough to make my teeth knock together and my heart jerk roughly in my chest.

I spin to see Nowicki scrambling away from

his locker as the mannequin falls stiffly to the ground, revealing the pink scrap of fabric threaded up the center of her crack-less ass.

"What the fuck?" Nowicki thumps a fist into his chest, his shoulders heaving as he continues to retreat across the room, which is now filled with rich laughter, Petrov's bass rumble, and Saunders weirdly high-pitched giggles. "What the unholy fuck, you fucks? Who put that in there?"

"Happy Rookie Prank Day." Justin claps his hands as he rises from the bench with a shit-eating grin. "God, you should see your face! You're even whiter than usual, Wickster."

"That's because I have a thing about mannequins, dude!" Nowicki scowls as he continues to thump his fist against his sternum, presumably to ensure his heart keeps beating. "It's a phobia, you asswipes."

His genuine rage sends a second wave of laughter through the rest of the team, all of whom suffered through their own rookie prank, most of which were messier and/or more disturbing than finding a mannequin stuffed in their locker. Suffice it to say, sympathy levels are low, though, when Nowicki's usually smooth voice breaks as he adds—

"I'm serious. I feel like I'm having a fucking heart attack just standing here looking at that thing."

—I almost feel bad about the part I played in the prank.

I'm the one who told Justin that Nowicki was terrified of mannequins, information gleaned from a heart-to-heart Nowicki and I had not long after he joined the team. Yes, it's a ridiculous fear, but we all have our own peculiar shit that trips us up for no reason other than our brains decide to get their wrinkles in a twist.

I don't have any phobias, but I've got my share of psychic baggage, enough that after Nowicki leaves the locker room in a huff, I refrain from following the rest of the team outside. If Nowicki is that upset about his locker, I don't want to see how he responds when he sees that his convertible is filled with four more mannequins, all dressed in lingerie and holding signs that read "We want to eat your face, Nowicki!"

Five years ago, I would have found a rookie's mannequin-phobia-induced meltdown as amusing as Jus and the rest of them, but I'm not that person anymore.

Now I'm thirty-two going on fifty, a single dad, and in over my head most of the time. Now I know what it feels like for my dreams to turn to dust in my mouth. I've lived with that taste since the day I got the call from the police about the accident, and nothing has been the same since.

Yes, I still laugh—usually at Chloe because my daughter, in addition to being my reason for living, is also hysterical—but I don't feel joy the way I used to.

But I don't hurt the way I did in the early days,

either. I don't get high, I don't get low, I get by. Get through. Get to the end of one day and brace myself for the start of another. And it is…good.

Good enough. Better than I thought it ever could be the morning I realized I'd lost Maryanne.

Still, there are moments, when I'm drifting off to sleep and mental stills of that long weekend with Laura drift through my head, reminding me of how close I got to something more than good enough, that I wish I wasn't such a rational son of a bitch. When I wish I believed that people could change and hearts could melt and reform into a different shape than they were before.

But wishes won't get you far in the real world, and that, unfortunately, is where I live, right at the intersection of Tough Truth Street and Not Meant to Be Boulevard.

Resigned to reality and its shittiness, I head for Laura's office to collect my daughter and beg for a favor I have no right to ask. But I'll ask anyway, because I'll do anything for Chloe, even cross lines I swore I would never step near again.

CHAPTER Two

Laura

If there's one thing I learned from years of babysitting as a teen, it's that it's a rare girl who can resist a makeup party. Tomboys, princesses, Star Wars nerds, dollhouse geeks, girls who rock out on drums, or girls who prefer quality time with books, they're all helpless against the temptation of an open cosmetic bag and an invitation to experiment on the canvas of the human face.

Chloe, who is already an accomplished artist, far more adept with pens, paints, and pastels at seven then I'll ever be at any age, is especially susceptible to the lure of powders, creams, and anything with sparkles in it.

"Oh, yes, Laura," she murmurs, a wicked grin curving her pink lips. "You're going to love this. You're really going to love it, I promise."

"I can't wait to see what you've done to me." I return her smile, though I have no doubt she's doing something awful to my face.

Chloe is going through a dark period in her artistic journey. A combination of tension with the teachers at her new school, nannies and babysitters who keep bailing without notice, and a disastrous trip to the waterfront to feed what turned out to be ninja attack seagulls has clouded her formerly cheery outlook on life. Gone are the cartoons of dragon princesses and happy frogs she used to love to draw—any excuse to use green and pink, her favorite colors, together—and in their place are disturbing portraits of murderous seagulls, goblins squatting beneath bridges, and a hissing cartoon creature of Chloe's own creation that she calls the Angry Garfbark.

It doesn't take a psych degree to figure out the child is not in her happy place.

If she were my kid, I would have pulled her out of that snotty private school the first week and told them to go fuck themselves if they aren't capable of seeing that Chloe is an incredible person worth taking the time to meet halfway. Not every child is going to respond to the same teaching style. Chloe needs time to daydream, draw, and be alone with her thoughts. Forcing her to engage with a group of twenty other kids all day long is exhausting for a serious introvert.

The past few times I've watched her for Brendan—after yet another nanny or babysitter called in sick at the last minute—Chloe has barely spoken a word for the first hour. She simply slouches in the overstuffed chair in the corner of my office, listlessly drawing the same cartoon animals over and over again.

She's exhausted from being shoved into a mold where she doesn't fit, and damn if I don't feel for the kid.

But I know better than to try to talk to Brendan again about my concerns. He appreciates my help with Chloe, but he's convinced the posh school is what's best for his daughter and that my opinion isn't worth listening to.

After all, I'm just a friend he fucked one weekend, not someone who matters…

"Don't move your face." Chloe presses a tiny finger between my eyebrows, rubbing back and forth until I relax the furrow there. "You're going to make me mess up."

"Yes, ma'am." I take a deep breath and force Chloe's dad from my thoughts.

I've been doing my best to keep my relationship with her separate from my often-strained relationship with Brendan, but it's not easy. Especially when I spend hours looking into sparkly blue eyes that are a mirror of her father's. She's a beautiful kid, as well as clever, sweet, and every bit as stubborn as her old man.

"How's your week going so far?" I ask, moving my lips as little as possible, in an effort to keep Chloe's canvas calm. "Pierce giving you any more trouble?"

"Yes!" Chloe's eyes suddenly go wide. "He's the worst! He showed everyone his butt yesterday!"

"What? Why did he do that?"

"He didn't want the girls to play soccer with the boys, so he pulled down his pants and showed his butt. It's called mooning, Seraphina said."

I nod sympathetically. "It is. But I didn't realize first graders were big into mooning each other."

"They're not. Just Pierce because he wanted us to run away. And we did, but it didn't matter. It was already too late. Once you've seen someone's butt, that's it. It's stuck in your brain forever."

"I hear you," I mumble. I've got my share of butts I would like to forget for various reasons—including her father's strong, sexy ass and how perfect it looked while he was walking away from me—but at least I didn't start collecting those mental images until I was a teenager. "So what happened after recess? Did Pierce get in trouble?"

Chloe shrugs as she exchanges the purple pencil for silver liquid eyeliner with sparkles—at least she's still into sparkles, giving me hope all is not gloom and doom between her little ears. "I don't know. He got sent to the counselor's office, so maybe. But he was back in class by snack time so it couldn't have been that bad."

I frown. "Well, if it happens again, tell me, and

I'll mention it to your dad. That's not the kind of thing that should happen more than once."

Chloe clucks her tongue. "Stop frowning. You're going to make this look crazy."

"I think you're responsible for the crazy. What are you doing to my face?"

She grins mysteriously. "You'll see. Now be still."

"Anyone ever tell you that you're bossy?"

Her grin becomes a giggle. "Yes. Dad. And Aunt Dee. And you. But you're bossy, too, so you can't complain."

"Oh, yeah?" My fingers dance across her ribs, making her laugh harder. "Is that how it works?"

"Yes," she gasps, squirming. "Now be good, Laura, or you're going to have to go for a time out!"

"Heck, no, I won't go!" I shout, giggling with her. A minute later, we're after each other's ribs—a mutually ticklish spot—and laughing so hard, we don't realize we're being observed until a sharp knock on the doorframe pulls our focus.

As soon as Chloe sees who's here, her face lights up. "Daddy!" A second later she's across the room, leaping into Brendan's arms.

"Hey, sweetheart." He hugs her tight, the love that softens his features making my heart twist. There's just something about seeing this big, tough man melt for his baby. It guts me every time, no matter how well I brace myself for the impact of seeing Brendan vulnerable, the way he was with me for those few short nights.

I swallow hard, banishing all soft, not-purely-friendly thoughts from my head before it's too late. I've just managed to get my feeling-fest under control when Brendan meets my gaze over Chloe's shoulder. His expression is pleasant, but guarded now, careful in a way I wish we didn't have to be careful with each other. "Hey, how was your afternoon?"

"Good," I say. "Chloe was an angel. As usual."

Chloe giggles wickedly in response, making both Brendan and I laugh. For a moment, his eyes dance into mine, and my heart does another aching, gravity-and-logic-defying flip.

I break eye contact, clearing my throat as I motion toward the floor near my desk. "Her backpack is right there, but I took her lunchbox down to the break room to wash it out. It's on the drying rack near the sink."

"I had an apple juice spill." Chloe pats Brendan's damp hair with a wrinkled nose. "Is this shower or sweat?"

"Shower, princess." He crosses the room, setting Chloe down near her bag. "I know how you feel about sweaty hair."

"Good." Chloe grabs her backpack and blows me a kiss. "Bye, Laura. See you next week."

"Bye, babes," I say with a smile. "Have a great long weekend. Eat lots of turkey and sweet potatoes for me."

"And pie," Chloe adds, giving me a thumbs-up

as she takes Brendan's hand. "Come on, Daddy, let's go. I'm hungry."

"Me, too," Brendan says, not moving. "But I need to talk to Laura. Can you do me a favor and go grab your lunchbox, and I'll meet you in the break room in five minutes?"

Chloe hesitates for a moment, gaze narrowing on his face. "You're not going to talk about me, are you? Because if you are, I want to be here, too."

Brendan smiles, but it's a more strained grin than I'm used to seeing when he's around his daughter. "No, I'm not going to talk about you. It's boring grownup stuff. Just give me five, okay? Then we'll get Thai food on the way home."

"Yay, summer rolls and veggie curry!" Chloe cheers before lunging forward to give me a big hug.

I hug her back, wondering if the hugs of a small person you adore ever get old—I'm thinking not. A second later, she's out the door, her pink high-tops slapping on the tile as she hurries toward the break room.

And then the Brendan-and-Laura-alone awkwardness descends with a heavy thud, the way it has since that weekend four months ago when I hinted that I wouldn't mind having feelings for Brendan if he would let me.

God, if only I could go back in time and suck those words back into my mouth, maybe I wouldn't feel so humiliated every time I'm alone with this man.

CHAPTER Three

Laura

I roll my eyes with a laugh, breaking the strained silence. "For a kid, that girl has an unnatural love of vegetables."

"She does. She keeps me healthy." He runs a hand through his damp hair, bringing my attention to the way his bicep bunches beneath his tight, navy sweater.

Don't, Laura.

Do not think about how good that arm felt wrapped around your waist. Do not think about how nice he smells or how pretty his eyes are or how much you would enjoy biting into him in about half a dozen places.

"So, anyway..." Brendan's gaze shifts to the wall behind me, where my cuckoo clock ticks softly. "Do you have a few minutes? I don't want to keep you if you've got somewhere to be."

"No. Nowhere to be." I rise from my comfy

chair to stand in front of him, feeling less vulnerable now that I only have to look up a few inches to meet his gaze—one of the advantages of being five foot nine. "What's up?"

"I have kind of a big favor to ask." He rubs the side of his neck, his thick fingers digging into the place where it meets his shoulder. "I normally wouldn't even consider bothering you with something like this, but it's for Chloe and—"

"You're not bothering me," I assure him. "I'm happy to watch her when you're in a bind. She's a great kid, and I have no problems getting my work done when she's here. She colors, I answer emails and make phone calls, and then we play." I shrug. "It's fun, actually. I enjoy her. She makes me laugh."

He nods, his lips curving softly. "Me, too." He sighs, his smile fading as his arm falls to his side. "But my favor isn't about watching her. Since school started, her grandparents have been riding my ass pretty hard about all the traveling I have to do and the effect it has on Chloe. And then, last week, they mentioned the possibility of Chloe moving in with them."

"What?" I blink faster. "Why?"

"They live in a small town near Mount Hood, with a great elementary school right down the street. And they're both retired, so they think they can provide a more stable home life for Chloe during the school year than I can, since I'm always traveling for games and practicing at weird hours and I can't seem to find a nanny who isn't a complete flake."

My brow furrows. "Dude. Your parents are pretty hardcore."

"Not my parents, Maryanne's. My mom and dad are still on Vancouver Island. Chloe only sees them a few times a year, but she talks to Steve and Angie all the time. They know she's been having a hard time adjusting to her new school, and they're worried about that. Among other things…" He props his hands low on his hips, his fingertips going white as they dig into the leather of his belt. "The other things are why I'm here."

I shake my head. "I'm sorry. I'm not following you."

His breath rushes out. "They think raising a kid isn't something a father can do alone—or at least, not do the way it's supposed to be done. Angie and Steve aren't happy that I haven't met someone, or at least started dating. They think three years is too long, and that I'm depriving Chloe of a female influence in her life."

I rock back on my heels. "Wow. That's heavy. And weird, at least from where I'm standing. I mean, Chloe's mom was their daughter. Isn't it kind of strange that they're in such a hurry for you to find a replacement?"

"It's not about that. It's about Chloe. She's all they care about." He paces toward my desk, shoulders creeping closer to his ears. "It's like they transferred all the love they had for Mary to

Chloe and now they're obsessed with making sure she has the perfect childhood. Or as perfect as it can be considering her mother died when she was three years old."

I blink and then blink again, but I'm still having a hard time wrapping my head around this.

If I died and left my husband and daughter alone, I would want him to move on and find love again, but I'm pretty sure my mother and father would be quite happy for my bereaved mate to remain a widower for the rest of his life. When it comes to my sister and me, my parents are blind to our failings. They only see the good stuff. I can't imagine them accepting a stepmom figure into their grandchild's life without a significant amount of pushback.

"It's getting so bad, I'm not sure they're going to be happy just riding my ass for much longer." He turns back to me, a haunted look in his eyes. "I think they're considering talking to a lawyer."

My jaw drops. "No way! They wouldn't! How could they even consider something like that? You're her father, and a damned good one."

"Thanks. But I'm not sure I'm good *enough* and I…" His lips press together, forming a pale seam at the bottom of his face before he continues in a softer voice, "I'm afraid I might lose her. That a judge could decide Steve and Angie are right and she's better off with them, and I just…" He clears his throat as he shakes his head. "I don't know what I'd do. I seriously don't know what I'd do without her."

I shouldn't touch him—that's not the nature of our relationship, and I promised myself I would keep my distance and preserve what's left of my pride—but I can't stop myself from stepping in and taking his stricken face in my hands. "You aren't going to lose her," I promise, heart breaking as I get an up close and personal look at the pain and worry in his eyes. "You aren't! No judge in his or her right mind would make that kind of call."

"And what if I get one that isn't in his or her right mind?"

I start to reassure him again but stop myself. As much as I would like to believe that any judge in Oregon would side with Brendan, I know that isn't true. Judges are just people—some of them are great at their job, some phone it in, some actively suck for one reason or another, and some are flat-out crazy.

The number of crazy people holding down jobs is a truly scary thing, and one of the reasons I hate to fly. Or go to the emergency room. Or eat sushi at an unfamiliar-to-me restaurant. Crazy people mopping the floors at the arena is one thing. Crazy strangers holding your life in their hands is quite another.

"So, what do you want me to do?" I brush my thumb softly back and forth across his stubble-rough cheek. "Talk to them? Promise to be a feminine influence in Chloe's life until you find a girlfriend?"

It's not a happy thought—I don't like to think about Brendan with another woman—but I'll do whatever it takes to take his pain away. Because that's what you do when you love someone, even if they don't love you back.

And Brendan would do the same for me if I had a friendly problem that needed solving, instead of a secret I-can't-get-over-our-fling-and-still-think-about-kissing-you-way-too-often problem. He has been infinitely more cooperative about PR opportunities since we burned our underwear together on the beach, and he spent an entire Sunday afternoon helping Justin—his teammate and our mutual friend—move my things into my new place a few weeks ago.

I can talk to his in-laws for him if that's what he needs. I'm already brainstorming all of the positive things I can say about his parenting, in fact, when he puts his hand over mine and says—

"I was hoping you would pretend to be my girlfriend. Just long enough to convince them that I'm sincerely looking for something real."

My thoughts go into stutter mode all over again, like a record catching on a scratch in a groove.

He's got to be fucking kidding me.

"I know." He takes my hands in his, curling his fingers around mine, drawing my knuckles down to rest against his chest. "It's a big favor, but you are my only friend who's also a woman and not already married. Which means you're my one shot at pulling this off. Steve and Angie know me, and if I bring a woman home for Thanksgiving who I don't have some sort of real relationship with, they'll know something's wrong."

My eyes open even wider. "You want me to go to your former in-laws with you for *Thanksgiving Day*?"

He winces, but that doesn't stop him from saying, "For the entire weekend, actually. Chloe and I usually stay four nights, since it's one of the few times a year when I know I won't have a game or practice."

"Four nights," I echo, laughing hysterically. "Oh my God. No! No, Brendan. I can't." I try to pull my hands from his, but he tightens his grip, sending a zing of awareness shooting up my arms.

"Please, Laura," he says, eyes burning into mine. "Please, say yes. If you do, I'll participate in every PR event from now until I retire. And I'll redo that nightmare bathroom in your new place so you don't have to wait for Justin to get around to helping you. I'm better with plumbing and laying tile, anyway."

"Brendan, please, it's not—"

"I'll get on my knees and beg if you want," he says, cutting me off. "Seriously, I'm begging you, Laura. I know this is a shitty thing to ask, but there isn't anyone else. If there were, I swear I would have asked her. You're my only hope here."

I swallow hard, willing myself not to glance down at his mouth, or think about all the things his full, sexy lips did to me while we were in bed together.

I fail, of course, because I am ridiculously weak when it comes to this man, and I'm experiencing some intense sensory recall involving his tongue and my nipple as I say in a husky voice, "It *is* a shitty thing to ask. And you know why."

The skin around his eyes tightens. "I know. I wouldn't have even considered it except that it's obvious you care about Chloe. And Chloe and I are a team. She needs me as much as I need her. Getting taken away from the only parent she has left isn't what's best for her, no matter what Steve and Angie think."

It's not. It would kill her, ravage that sweet, artistic soul I love, and I can't let that happen. Even if pretending to be her dad's girlfriend is going to be like having my heart pecked out of my chest by a pack of those seagulls she hates so much.

"What are you going to tell her?" I ask, wanting to get that sorted out before I give him an answer. "I don't want to confuse her or lie to her."

"I don't, either. But I want to lose her even less. I figure if we tell her that we're special friends that should be okay. She already knows we're close."

"Special friends, huh?" I arch a brow, surprised by how stiff my skin feels.

I reach up to scratch my forehead and come away with a purple and black fingernail, remembering too late that I never got a look at what Chloe did to me.

I reach around Brendan, grabbing the mirror from my desk, only to screech and nearly drop it when I see a witch with purple eyebrows reaching up to her hairline staring back at me. "Oh my God! Why didn't you tell me I'm terrifying?"

Brendan's lips curve. "I assumed you knew."

"No, I didn't know!" I swipe my box of makeup remover wipes from beside the mirror and pop it open. "That kid of yours has a future in special effects. I barely recognize myself."

I realize that the entire time I've been thinking sexy thoughts about Brendan, I've looked like a witch and a goblin got together to spawn an ugly redheaded, purple-faced baby, and blush. "How could you have a serious conversation with me when I look like this?"

His smile softens. "You look like that because you were making my little girl happy."

Well, shit…

And *sigh*…

There it is again—that loving, devoted daddy side of Brendan that makes my ovaries explode. I am helpless against it. Every ounce of my tough, take-no-prisoners, refuse-to-put-up-with-any-bullshit side melts into a puddle of *aw* every time I'm confronted with the clear evidence of how much he adores his daughter.

"Fine," I mumble, rubbing a wet wipe against my cheek.

His eyes light up. "Is that a yes?"

"Yes. But you're going to owe me." I hold a warning hand up between us, wanting to make sure he understands this is a big fucking deal. "Seriously. My parents aren't going to be happy about me canceling last minute, especially since this is our first holiday together as a family since Libby and Justin became more than friends. My sister probably isn't going to be happy, either. Libby and I have pulled the wishbone every year since she was old enough to hold on to her side, and she's very into honoring family traditions."

Brendan's lips part, but he apparently rethinks whatever he was going to say and simply nods. "Right. I understand. Anything you want. Thank you, Laura. I appreciate this. So much. You have no idea."

He reaches for me, and for a second I think he's going to pull me in for a hug, but instead, he wraps his fingers around my shoulders and squeezes for a second or two before letting me go and backing away. "I'll text you tonight, and we can iron out the details. I should get Chloe before she finds the candy stash in the break room."

"Oh, she found that weeks ago." I pluck a

fresh wipe from my box—my first one is already deep black and purple. "I've had to move it twice. But this time it's hidden where not even a gummy bear bloodhound will be able to find it."

Brendan smiles. "Thanks."

"I only hid it because I'm selfish and don't like to share my gummy bears," I lie, pretending I don't know damned well that he monitors Chloe's sugar intake like a scientist tracking seismic vibrations on the San Andreas fault.

"I meant thanks for saying yes," he says, his eyes doing the sexy sparkling thing they did that night on the beach. "You're good people, Freckles."

"Yeah, yeah," I grumble, pretending my ribs aren't squeezing my heart into a squishy, maudlin lump of longing in my chest. "Go get your kid. I'll see you tomorrow. And bring coffee and donuts. I'm a shitty girlfriend—real or fake—if I'm not regularly fed and caffeinated."

He brings two fingers to his temple in a mock salute. "Yes, ma'am."

And then he's gone, and I'm left to wipe away the last of my witch face in peace, and wonder what the hell I've done.

CHAPTER Four

From the texts of Laura Collins
and Libby Collins

Laura: Are you awake?

Libby: It's only nine o'clock. Of course I'm awake.

Laura: Well, I can never tell anymore. Since you and Justin started getting domesticated, it seems like you're asleep by eight-thirty every night.

Libby: In bed and sleeping are two very different things, big sister dear…

Laura: Ew. So gross.
I don't want to hear about you and Justin getting it on, Elizabeth.
I've known him since we were twelve. I watched

him pick his nose and wipe it on his desk in sixth grade. He's basically a disgusting, goober dork. And no amount of muscle, handsomeness, fame, skill, or two-hundred-dollar jeans can change that.

Libby: Well, we can't all be perfect by age twelve. And I'm pretty sure he uses tissues now.

Laura: Or so you think. You should set up a nanny cam to film him while he's watching television alone. I bet he still does totally gross stuff.

Libby: I thought you were okay with Justin and I being together, La.
I thought you approved. Am I missing something?

Laura: No. I approve. I'm glad you're in love and that he makes you happy.
But that doesn't mean I'm going to stop ripping on him. He seduced my baby sister without permission. He owes me three more major favors before he'll be allowed back in my good graces.

Libby: Oh good! He thought he was on the hook for at least five or six more.

Laura: Nah. I'm going soft in my old age.
I'm probably also going crazy...
I just agreed to be Brendan's fake girlfriend for

the weekend to help get his former in-laws off his back.

Libby: What?!

Laura: Apparently they think he needs to start dating and have been making a big stink about him providing a "female influence" for Chloe. So I agreed to help him out.
Are you okay with making my excuses to Mom and Dad?
I would call Mom myself, but she'll keep me on the phone forever, and I have to pack for a long weekend with several nice dinners and skiing involved. Which means I basically have to pack my entire closet, plus extra long-johns and every pair of socks I own.

Libby: How about I tell them you're not feeling well?
That way no one gets upset.

Laura: But then Mom will try to bring me turkey soup on Friday and freak out when I'm not home. Just tell them I'm doing a top secret, urgent favor for a friend and that I'll explain everything next week, okay?

Libby: Okay, but is it really that urgent? Couldn't you meet Brendan on Friday, instead? I miss you. I feel like we haven't had a chance to get our gossip on lately.

Laura: And whose fault is that Miss In Bed Banging Her Boyfriend By Eight Thirty Every Night?

Libby: *blushing smiley face emoji*
Sorry, it's like a new toy. A really exciting new toy…

Laura: It's okay. I get it.
We'll catch up in a month or two when the sex fog starts to clear.

Libby: Will it start to clear by then? God, I hope so.
I mean, I love being with Justin, don't get me wrong, but it's like all I can think about is sex. Sex in the shower, sex on the drive to school, sex while I'm grading papers and whipping up fresh batches of play dough and picking glue out of my hair. My mind is in the gutter pretty much twenty-four seven, Laura.
I'm beginning to think I have a problem…

Laura: But what a problem to have, right? *winking emoji*

Libby: LOL. Hmmm. Yes. Things could definitely be worse.
Have a Happy Thanksgiving, and don't worry

about Mom and Dad. I'll keep them off your back until next week.

Laura: Thank you so much.
Night-night, nympho.

Libs: Night-night. *blushing smiley face emoji*

From the texts of Laura Collins and Chloe Daniels

Chloe: Dad told me you're coming with us for Thanksgiving at Gammy and Pop Pop's house!!!!! I'm so excited!!!! We're going to have so much fun!
I can show you all my toys! I have so many toys at their house!
Dad says they spoil me rotten!!!

Laura: LOL. You aren't rotten, but you are a mess.
Thanks for the goblin witch makeover, by the way…

Chloe: HAHAHA!! You're welcome!!
You were so scary!!!
Did you take a picture?
I forgot I wanted a picture to add to my art book!

Laura: No, I didn't take a picture.

Chloe: Oh well, I can do it again. I remember what colors I used.
I can do your makeup in the car on the way to Gammy's house and we can show her when we get there!!

Laura: How about we wait and do a redo next week?
I would kind of like to meet your grandparents looking like myself, you know?
Not a crazy monster person with eyebrows up to my hairline…

Chloe: HAHAHA!!
So scary!! I'm going to have nightmares about your face!!!
HAHAHAHA!!!

Laura: All right, crazy head. Get to bed, and I'll see you tomorrow.
Can't wait to eat pie for breakfast with you this weekend!

Chloe: Me, too!! *pie emoji* *heart emoji* *heart emoji*

> From the texts of Brendan Daniels and Laura Collins

Brendan: I saw Chloe texted you. As you can

probably tell, she's pretty excited. I think she's finally asleep, but she was bouncing off the walls when I first told her you were coming with us.

Laura: Oh, good! I'm glad.
So she wasn't weirded out by the "special friends" thing?

Brendan: Not at all. But kids are like that.
They ask a lot fewer questions than adults do.

Laura: Except when they're asking all the questions.
Like about how many seconds there are in a year or why toilets flush backward in Australia or how armadillos can infect people with leprosy.

Brendan: Right. Kids are all about the hard-hitting questions.
Thanks for your help with the leprosy thing, by the way. Chloe finally took her stuffed armadillo out of quarantine in the guest bathroom.

Laura: My pleasure. It was a fascinating afternoon of Internet research.
I now know more about armadillos and leprosy than I ever imagined possible.

Brendan: Speaking of imagining things…
I've been thinking about how this weekend is going to play out…

Laura: Yes?

Brendan: I mean, I don't think there's any reason to overdo it, since Chloe's going to be underfoot and Steve and Angie are my former in-laws...
But if we're not at least a little...affectionate they aren't going to buy that we're more than friends.

Laura: Okay...
So, what does that mean?

Brendan: Kissing. Holding hands, maybe.
And sleeping in the same room. In the same bed. Steve and Angie aren't old-fashioned people. Steve is a former biologist and Angie taught teen health and sex ed for thirty years, so...
What do you think? Is that all right with you?

Laura: Of course. It's no big deal.
I mean, it's not like we haven't kissed before...

Brendan: Right. About that...
I'm sorry I was so abrupt the morning I left the hotel. I've felt bad about it ever since, I just haven't known how to apologize for something like that.

Laura: Ground rule number one, and only for this weekend: we don't talk about last summer.
It's over, and we've been doing great with the friends thing. It's fine. There's no need to rehash

it all and make things weird. We'll pull off a few sweet kisses in front of your former in-laws, sleep platonically in the same bed, and then come home and get back to friendship as usual.
Done. Easy. No stress.

Brendan: Okay. Sounds good. Thank you.
So, we'll pick you up at 7 a.m.? With coffee and donuts?

Laura: Perfect. Good night.

Brendan: Good night. And I really do appreciate this so much, Laura.
I'm glad it's not going to be weird.

Laura: Ditto

From Laura's journal

Tomorrow I'm leaving to spend four days pretending to be Brendan's girlfriend.

AND IT'S GOING TO BE SO FUCKING WEIRD! ARGH! WHY DID I EVER SAY YES TO THIS STUPID, WEIRD PLAN? IT'S SO STUPID! AND WEIRD!

Note to self: Stop saying yes to stupid, weird plans. Stop saying yes to anything, in fact, until you get your head on straight and stop doing dumb things like crushing on a man who is never going to be more than a friend.

Ugh. Stupid. Weird. Blah...

See you on Monday, journal. Keep it tight.

CHAPTER Five

Brendan

So weird.

This is going to be so fucking weird, but I don't have a choice. I just need to forget that I memorized the exact sweet, salty flavor of Laura's skin, and the way she moves when she's pinned to the sheets beneath me, and the sexy sounds she makes when she's about to come on my fingers.

Or my mouth.

Or my cock, with her long legs wrapped around my waist and her fingers digging into my shoulders and her body so hot and tight it feels like I've died and gone to heaven.

I swallow hard, gritting my teeth as I turn onto her street.

Hell. I'm going to be in hell, and it's my own damned fault. I should never have slept with

Laura in the first place. I'm a grown man, for God's sake. I know better than to start something with someone I work with, someone I'll be forced to run into every day when things don't work out.

Like you gave it a chance to work out.

You thought you were being so smart, heading heartache off at the pass. But all you did was screw yourself and ensure Laura thinks you're a jackass.

I curse beneath my breath, and Chloe pipes up from the backseat, "I heard that! You have to put a dollar in the swear jar when we get home."

I'm tempted to curse again—if this isn't a morning for swearing like a damned sailor, I don't know what is—but instead, I offer a terse, "Got it. Sorry, honey," and reach over to turn up the radio.

I'm never going to convince my seven-year-old to stop pushing her swearing boundaries if I can't get control of my own mouth. And the last thing I need is for Chloe to start exercising her locker room vocabulary in front of Angie and Steve. I need to prove that I'm a fit parent with my shit together, not further the impression that I'm getting by on a wing and prayer and more help from my friends than any thirty-two-year-old man with six figures in his savings account should need.

But money can't buy everything, and lately that's included reliable childcare.

Portland is experiencing a serious nanny and

babysitter shortage. If Justin and Laura hadn't stepped in to help me out half a dozen times each, I don't know what I would have done. In Justin's case, I don't feel too bad—I've done my share of favors for Jus in the years we've been friends—but with Laura...

Well, with Laura I feel like a bastard.

A seriously shitty excuse for a human being who made love to her like it was my mission on Earth for three days, told her I wasn't interested in feelings because I needed stability for my daughter, and then proceeded to take advantage of her generosity and hit her up for childcare assistance in my time of need. And now I've put her in an even worse spot with the fake-girlfriend shit, when all of this could have been avoided if I hadn't been so damned convinced that she was secretly in love with my best friend.

In my defense, Justin and Laura have one of those weirdly close friendships that look a lot like repressed attraction. They party all summer on his boat, have movie nights every other week, laugh way too loud when they're together, and hug good-bye with an intensity that makes it clear that they love each other.

But they don't love each other in *that* way.

Justin loves Laura's little sister, Libby, in *that* way, and Laura seems genuinely happy that Jus and Libby have found something special together.

Which means I'm an idiot.

I'm a fool who botched my shot at being the

man in Laura's bed because I was so certain I was a distraction, a placeholder, something to settle for until she and Jus found their way through friendship to something more. Because I woke up that last morning in Cannon Beach with her lying next to me, looking so beautiful it was painful to lay eyes on her, and decided I would rather have nothing than be second best.

By the time I realized how wrong I was, it was too late. I'd already hurt Laura's feelings, wounded her pride, and wrecked any chance I might have had with her. Since that weekend, every time we're together, Laura's walls go up so fast it gives me whiplash. The only time I see the soft, silly, vulnerable woman I held hands with on the beach is when she's with Chloe.

Laura clearly adores my daughter. And Chloe adores her. And fuck if that doesn't shove the knife deeper every time I see Chloe hug Laura good-bye.

Now, as I pull onto Sherman Street, spotting the willowy redhead in a white sweater, and jeans that hug her phenomenal ass waiting for me at the end of her driveway with a determined but distant smile fixed on her face, it's all I can do not to keep driving. I don't want an awkward weekend with fake kisses and a line of pillows stacked between us to make sure I stay on my side of the bed. I want the chance I screwed up last summer.

But I should know by now that what I want

doesn't matter.

"Laura!" The moment I shut off the car, Chloe erupts from the backseat, lunging at Laura and hugging her tight. "Ride in the backseat with me! I brought car trip bingo! We can play the whole way there!"

"Sounds awesome," Laura says, the warmth in her eyes cooling as her gaze shifts my way. "Good morning."

"Good morning." I slam the door closed and motion to the large suitcase and smaller travel bag at the end of the driveway. "This all your gear?"

"Yeah. Sorry. Once you introduced skiing into the mix, the packing situation got out of hand."

"No worries. We've got plenty of room." I pop open the back of the Land Cruiser and slide Laura's luggage in beside Chloe's. By the time I'm done, Laura has buckled Chloe into her car seat and is circling around the front of the SUV to the passenger's side.

"You don't mind if I ride in back, do you?" she asks as I move to meet her. "You and I will have plenty of forced togetherness once we get to your in-laws' house."

"Right." My throat goes tight as I scan her face, looking for a weakness in her defenses, but not finding a single crack. In fact, she looks even less thrilled to see me than usual.

Steve and Angie might not notice her standoffishness, at least not right away, but I certainly do, and with every passing second, I'm growing less certain that we'll be able to pull this off.

This isn't the woman I kissed on the beach. This isn't the woman I tucked under my arm as I fell asleep, or woke with a trail of kisses up the sweet, soft skin of her inner thigh. This woman practically radiates "Don't Even Think About Touching Me, Creep" vibes. I can't imagine that kissing her is going to feel anything but forced and awkward, and that's not going to slip by a former sex ed teacher unnoticed.

"You okay?" Laura arches a brow, hesitating beside the door.

"No, I'm not." My fingers cover hers, stopping her before she can pull the handle. "I need to know something before we leave."

"Okay," she says, with a frown. "Are you sure you're—"

Her words end in a hum of surprise as I wrap my arm around her waist, pulling her against me as my mouth finds hers.

And for a moment, it's as awkward as I feared it would be. Her lips are stiff, and she's gone so rigid it feels like I'm wrapping my arms around one of the statues at the botanical gardens. But when my tongue sweeps out to tease the seam of her mouth, she softens. Her lips part and she melts against me, her arms going around my neck as I stroke deep into her mouth, tasting mint toothpaste and the darker, sweeter taste of Laura.

She tastes like secrets whispered beneath the

covers, and spices I don't know the names for, and places I've never been but really, *really* want to visit. She makes me ache in a way I didn't think I would ever ache again, and all I want to do is carry her into the house, up to her bedroom, and make love to her until all her walls come tumbling down.

But my daughter is here, in the backseat, a fact I'm reminded of when a sharp knock on the window makes Laura jump, and her teeth knock lightly against mine.

"Ouch." She laughs and tries to step away, but I tighten the arm encircling her waist, keeping her warm, curvy body close to mine.

A moment later, Chloe shoves open the door and sticks her head into the cool winter air. "Hey!" Her wide eyes flick from me to Laura and back again. "Since when did you two start kissing?"

"Since this summer." I mix truth in with the lie, in case Steve and Angie start asking Chloe questions when I'm not around. Better that they think Laura and I have been together for a while and this relationship isn't a flash in the pan.

"Oh." Chloe's gaze narrows, but after a second she nods. "Okay."

"Okay?" Laura asks, blinking. "That's it?"

"I mean, it's kind of embarrassing," Chloe says with a grin. "But I know about boyfriends and girlfriends. Seraphina has a boyfriend. He gives her his dessert at lunch."

"I would give Laura my dessert," I say. "Any time she asked for it."

Laura clears her throat as she pats my chest. "That's okay. You can keep your dessert. We've got donuts, and I'm sure there's going to be plenty of pie around this weekend. But shouldn't we get going? Didn't you say it's around a two-hour drive?"

I nod. "Yeah. We should get going. Buckle up, Chloe."

"Okay, but Laura's still riding in back with me, Dad. I called her first."

"Noted." I smile, Laura's lips curve in response, and for the first time since last summer, I spy a break in the fortress she's built to keep me out.

"Hey," I add in a softer voice as Chloe crawls back to her car seat. "Sorry to spring that on you. I just wanted to be sure we could be convincing."

"It's fine." She brushes her hair over her shoulder, clearing her throat. "But you don't have to worry. I took drama classes in college. I can fake being head-over-heels for a weekend, no problem."

"Good," I say. But the chilly note in her voice feels the opposite of good, and the moment she steps out of my arms and slides into the backseat feels even worse.

But then, no one ever said being a single parent was going to be easy.

That's what I have to do—stay focused on this

SEXY MOTHERPUCKER

as something I'm doing as a parent, to keep Chloe with me where she belongs, and ignore the voice in my head that suggests it might not be too late to convince the other redhead in my life to give me another chance.

Chapter Six

Laura

By the time I'm able to stop thinking about The Kiss—the devastatingly sexy, intense, panty-melting kiss—we're miles outside the city, zipping toward the greater Mount Hood ski area along roads lined with snow-dusted farms and cozy cottages instead of urban sprawl.

Chloe is kicking my ass in road-trip bingo, but that's fine. Chloe likes to win, and I'm grateful for an excuse to stare out the window and pretend to be looking for "No U-turn" signs, cows, police cars, joggers, and the other items on my card. But I'm not looking for joggers, and I miss at least two chances to cover my cow space with a tiny blue magnet—according to Chloe, who takes great delight in pointing out my lost opportunity.

All I'm thinking is….

Shit!

SEXY MOTHERPUCKER

Shit, shit, shit! What have you gotten yourself into?

Seriously? What have you done? And how are you going to keep from melting into a pathetic puddle of lust at Brendan's feet and begging him to put your pussy out of its misery before the weekend is through?

Until Brendan kissed me this morning, I was pretty sure that shacking up at his former wife's parents' house would be enough to put a serious damper on the attraction I feel for the man. It's a sad, strange situation and only seemed stranger the longer I lay awake in bed last night, fretting about my ability to pull off pretending to be Brendan's special lady friend in front of strangers.

But now...

I steal a glance at the driver's seat, and my pulse immediately throbs faster.

Even his profile is stunning. But it isn't the strong jaw with the dusting of stubble, the perfectly balanced features, or the full lips that make my heart flip and my chest ache. It's the man himself—this man I long for and loathe in equal measure.

I *hate* that he kissed me and reminded me how intense the chemistry is between us. And I *love* that he kissed me, giving me another chance to memorize how electric it feels to be in his arms.

If nothing else, at least this trip will give me fresh fantasy fodder for the months ahead, fuel for more long nights spent with my vibrator, trying not to think about Brendan. Nights that inevitably end with me replaying scenes from our hot-as-hell weekend over and over again in my mind as Bob, my battery-operated boyfriend, buzzes his sad, lonely, one-noted tune between my legs.

Ugh! I'm so pathetic.

I should have fucked Brendan out of my system a long time ago.

Back in September, I should have taken Hot Goatee Guy from happy hour at the Knock Back Bar home and ridden him all night long. Or I should have called Nelson, my college boyfriend, who's always up for a random hookup when we're both single and feeling sad. Hell, I might have been better off if I'd accepted one of Henry's many apologies for borrowing my underwear without asking and gotten back with my ex for a few months.

Henry would have been on his best behavior, reminding me why I had a soft spot for the big, power-lifting, panty-robbing idiot in the first place, and my heart would have released its death grip on the idea of Brendan and me becoming more than friends.

Because that's all it is—an idea. A fantasy.

The reality is that Brendan is using me. Yes, I'll be in a place to demand remodeling favors or anything else I want from him as soon as this weekend is over, but still…

I feel used.

And yucky.

And sad.

"Laura, you really are hopeless," Chloe says, patting me on the leg.

I'm momentarily terrified that I've muttered something I was thinking aloud. But then, Chloe smiles and holds out her Bingo card. "Here, take mine and I'll take yours. At this rate I'm going to beat you before we get to Boring, and that's no fun."

"Boring?" I hand over my nearly empty card with an apologetic grimace.

"It's a town. We stop on the way to Thanksgiving every year," Brendan offers from the front seat. It's the first time he's spoken since we left Portland, making me think I'm not the only one who feels like they're marinating in pure awkwardness.

At least Chloe seems oblivious. Thank God.

The last thing I want to do is confuse the kid any more than she's going to be confused once Brendan and I have to explain, somewhere down the line, why we've decided to stop kissing.

"And I get a T-shirt for my Boring T-shirt collection," Chloe says, kicking her pink sneakers. "Last year it was 'Boring! What an exciting place to live!' This year I want to get the one with the sister city cartoons on it."

"Dull, Scotland, and Bland, New South Wales, are the sister cities," Brendan explains, making me laugh.

"Well, of course. They would be." I glance up, catching Brendan watching me in the rearview mirror with an odd look on his face. Before I can figure out what the look means, his gaze is back on the road and he's jabbing a finger toward the passenger's side window. "Out there, Laura. Cows at three o'clock."

"Daddy, stop, that's cheating!" Chloe scowls at the back of Brendan's head. "And besides, the cows are on my card now. I took Laura's and she took mine. So you're just messing up everything!"

"Aw, give him a break," I say, a little surprised. I've never heard Chloe take such a hard line with Brendan before. She's usually in full hero-worship mode when her dad's around. "He was just trying to help."

"Cheating isn't helping." Chloe transfers her glare to me. "It isn't right and it's against the rules."

"Chloe has a thing about games and rules," Brendan says. "Violations of rules bring out her bad side."

Chloe harrumphs. "I don't have a bad side. *You* have a bad side. Laura said so."

My jaw drops. "What? I did not!"

"You did, too. You told Libby you were watching me because Daddy gets cranky if he has to be nice to people and look after me at the same time."

I press my lips together, biting back the curse on the tip of my tongue. *Damn it.* I *did* say that. "Okay, you're right. But in my defense, that was six months ago, and you were wearing headphones at the time. I thought I was safe."

"You're never safe with this one. She's always listening." Brendan's eyes crinkle. "And don't worry about it. I am cranky sometimes."

I shake my head, flustered by his grin, even in a reflection. "True, but I'm still sorry. I never meant for Chloe to hear that."

"It's okay." Chloe plucks a blue magnet from the open Bingo kit between us. "I've heard worse. Sometimes Daddy and Justin forget I'm watching television in the locker room, and Justin has a really bad potty mouth. He says the eff-word all the time. Oh, U-turn sign! One more for me."

"Okay, that's it." I hold up my blue magnet. "This is about to get serious. You're going down, Chloe. I feel a rest stop sign coming up any second now. Bingo is so close I can taste it."

She giggles. "I don't think so, but you can try."

I force myself to pay attention to the game—much better than paying attention to the confusing, angst-inducing man in the front seat—but when we reach the exit for Boring ten minutes later, Chloe has Bingoed twice, and I still haven't filled a single row.

At the tourism center, I slide out of the backseat into the chilly air, shaking my head and wondering if I have undiagnosed ADHD. I have twenty years and a college degree on Chloe. Surely I should be able to hold my own in a game of Bingo.

"Come on, Laura!" Chloe dashes for the door

to the center, waving her hand urgently for me to follow. "I'll show you which shirts I already have in my collection."

"Be right there," I promise, fetching my sock hat from my purse and tugging it down over my ears.

"Don't feel bad." Brendan pauses near the front of the Cruiser to wait for me.

"I can't help it. She kicked my butt. Hard. And the past fifteen minutes I was actually trying."

He grins, his eyes glacier-blue and lovely in the morning light. "I meant about saying I was a cranky bastard. But don't feel bad about Bingo, either. We drive this route five or six times a year. She has the signs memorized. She knew when she gave you her card that you weren't going to be able to find a Bingo. It was a trap disguised as generosity."

"That little sneak!" I cast an incredulous look toward the center, but the windows are reflective. I can't see Chloe inside.

All I can see is a ridiculously handsome man in a thick brown sweater and jeans that are tight across the thighs, giving testimony to the powerful body hidden beneath his clothes, and a slim redhead with skin nearly the same shade as her white sweater and an oversize pom-pom sticking up above her head, making her look like an upside-down albino exclamation point.

Lord, I am out of my league with this man.

Even if he didn't have a child and

responsibilities he thinks I'm not equipped to handle, it would never work. I'm a 6—maybe a 7 on days when I've had a blow-out and time to devote to makeup—who earns enough to pay my bills. Brendan is a 10—9 on days when he makes scowling his full-time job—and his Cruiser costs more than I make in an entire year. He's a famous professional athlete who owns a string of steakhouses and appears in local and national commercials for various companies that are willing to pay him big bucks to put his face, fame, and reputation behind their products. My sphere of influence includes the two women who work beneath me in the PR department and a few college interns I get to bully for a semester or two before they move on to bigger and better things.

We're about as well matched as a rhino and one of those birds that hang out on their backs eating ticks.

But that wouldn't matter if there were feelings involved. Love forgives a multitude of sins, and it couldn't care less about money or fame. Or ticks.

And if you think about it, the rhino is probably pretty grateful not to be covered in blood-sucking arachnids.

But there aren't feelings involved here. Not even affection, let alone love. It's a fact I need to keep at the forefront of my mind at moments like this, when Brendan is smiling at me like he might care about my emotional well-being.

"She is a sneak sometimes." He glances over his shoulder. "And she has a temper. Especially when she doesn't sleep well. She was up three times last night asking for water before I finally got her settled."

I shrug. "That's okay. Sometimes I have a temper, too."

"Maybe it's a redhead thing." He reaches out, curling a lock of my hair around his finger, bringing his hand so close to my breast that my nipples tighten for reasons that having nothing to do with the chill in the air.

They're tight because I want him to touch me, kiss me. Because I want to feel his mouth on my skin and the muscles of his thighs, thick and strong against mine, as he nudges my legs apart and settles between them. I want him on top of me, moving inside of me, his breath hot on my lips, stealing mine away.

For a moment, the need to touch him, to connect with this person who made me feel things that before our weekend on the beach I didn't know were possible, is so strong that I sway forward, an iron filing helpless to resist the pull of a big, sexy, manly magnet. But before I can do something stupid like wrap my arms around Brendan's neck or push up on tiptoe to press my lips to his, Chloe bursts back through the Visitor's Center door.

"Can I have an orange soda?" she asks, hopping with excitement. "They have the kind in the glass bottle that I like."

Brendan turns, my hair slipping through his

fingers as he steps away. "No soda before lunch, and definitely no soda on a day when you've already had a donut and plan to have pie."

"But it's my favorite!" she protests, freckled nose wrinkling as Brendan crosses to meet her. "I could have half of it."

"No."

She takes his hand with wide, pleading eyes. "Just a few drinks?"

"No."

"One drink?" she wheedles. "And then I can save the rest for tomorrow?"

"No," he says again, reminding me of our conversations pre-underwear-burning. The man really does love saying no.

And he's very, *very* good at it.

"You could learn something here, woman," I mutter as I follow them into the building, wishing all over again that I had said "no" to this favor instead of "yes."

Because at this rate it's not a question of *if* I'll make a lovesick fool of myself in front of Brendan this weekend, but when.

CHAPTER Seven

Brendan

I pride myself on my discipline and self-restraint.

I rarely cheat on the diet my nutritionist designed to keep me functioning at peak potential as I move out of my drink-beer-and-eat-pizza-and-still-kill-it-on-the-ice twenties and into my have-to-work-twice-as-hard-to-maintain-game-shape mid-thirties. I never skip leg day—or arm day, or ab day—and I give everything on the ice, whether it's an optional skate, mandatory practice, a mid-season snoozer of a game, or the final battle of the playoffs.

I maintain firm but fair boundaries for my daughter, and ensure she's eating well and getting enough sleep. I'm equally fair as a team captain, choosing positive reinforcement and constructive, privately-delivered criticism over a raised voice or a brutal come-down on a floundering rookie in front of his new team. I take my supplements religiously, watch YouTube videos until I master whatever French braid is in style this week at Chloe's school, book a massage with the team trainer every Wednesday to keep my bum shoulder functioning smoothly, and clip Chloe's nails every other Thursday night.

I am structured, dedicated, focused, and in control of myself, my team, and my household.

But right now, all I want to do is drop Chloe off at her grandparents' house, drive back to Government Camp as fast as the Cruiser can go on the windy mountain roads, book a hotel room, and shack up with Laura for the next two or three weeks, shirking all of my responsibilities and committing myself solely to the study of the art of getting her off.

The two-hour drive has done absolutely fuck all to take off the edge, probably because I've spent most of it mentally replaying scenes from our stolen weekend.

A particular favorite is of Laura's lips parting and her eyes sliding closed as I roll my tongue against her clit, increasing my pressure until she arches into my mouth and I drive my tongue deep into her pussy, needing to feel her body pulse as she comes for me. Because of me. Because I've brought this strong, sexy, in-control woman to her knees.

And then there's Laura with her shirt

unbuttoned in the moonlight, holding my gaze as she straddles me on the chair we dragged out onto the deck so we could listen to the waves crash while we went for round five. Images of my hands parting the fabric of her white button-up and cupping her breasts, of her reaching between us and fitting my swollen length to where she is already hot and ready for me, so ready that the moment we glide together is pure bliss, pure relief, perfection unlike anything I've felt in so long.

And then we start to move, my cock stroking deep inside her. Deeper, deeper, as our eyes meet and hold and fucking becomes something more. Something true and right and so intense that by the time we finally reach the edge together I can barely breathe. My lungs are locked tight, and my heart is pounding, and I'm so lost in Laura that all I can do is wrap my arms around her and wait for the world to stop spinning and my soul to slip back into my skin.

It's that moment—the moment when I realized that I was making love to Laura, not just fucking away the loneliness—that pulses through my mind again and again, inspiring an erection so intense that, after I pull into Steve and Angie's driveway, I have to take a moment to talk myself down before I get out of the truck.

Fuck. What the hell is wrong with me?

This is the house where I used to spend holidays with my wife and my newborn child.

And while I know that it's healthy, even necessary, to move on after loss, and three years is probably more than sufficient time to wait before starting a new relationship, that isn't what's happening here.

What's happening is that I've got a completely inappropriate hard-on for the *friend* who agreed to help me fool my in-laws, deceiving them into backing off and leaving me be. A friend who clearly has no interest in letting me close to her body again, let alone her heart.

Which means I need to get my head on straight and stop dwelling on the past.

Exhaling with the same intensity as that moment before I take to the ice for a game, I push out of the Cruiser, waving at Steve and Angie, who are already halfway down the drive.

"Hello, hello!" Angie, looking like the consummate grandma in a poinsettia sweater and khakis, topped by a "Gimme Some Sugar" apron the same gray as her shoulder-length hair, holds out both arms, aiming her slim body at Laura, who smiles widely and leans down to accept a way-too-enthusiastic hug. "You must be Laura, we're so pleased to meet you! And you're so beautiful! Look, Steve, look how beautiful she is."

"Beautiful," Steve echoes, reaching out to pat me on the back as he meets me at the rear of the truck. "We appreciate redheads around here."

"I had red hair when I was younger," Angie confides with a laugh.

"And I'm a redhead," Chloe crows, running past Angie into the house. "Come on, Laura, come see my toys!"

"She'll be there in just a second," Angie calls over her shoulder. "Don't rush us. We need to say a proper hello." She turns back, beaming up at Laura as she takes her hand and pats it like a beloved pet, overdoing it every bit as much as I feared she would.

But at least Laura should be prepared. I warned her before we left the tourism center that my in-laws are genuinely effusive people.

"Now, tell me all about yourself," Angie continues. "Brendan says you work for the Badgers. That must be so much fun. We love hockey. Catch a game at least four times a year, even though the drive home from the city at night isn't Steve's favorite. Brendan tries to get us to stay the night at his house, but I need my own bed. Can't sleep a wink when I'm in a strange place."

"Unless it's that fancy hotel they opened on the other side of the mountain." Steve winks as he helps me pull the bags out of the back of the Cruiser.

"Well, that's another story," Angie says with a guilty grin. "I do love a room with a mountain view. And room service for breakfast. Speaking of breakfast, have you all eaten? The turkey won't be ready until two, but I've got quiche to warm up, or we could start the holiday off right with pie."

"We've eaten, but I'm sure Chloe will be up for pie." Laura follows Angie up the walk. "She's been bragging about her Gammy's pies for weeks."

Angie nods seriously. "They really are quite good. I want us to be friends, Laura, so I won't start things off on the wrong foot by being falsely modest about my pies."

Laura laughs. "Good. Why should women play down our accomplishments while men get to brag all they want?"

Angie glances over her shoulder at me, her pale blue eyes widening with excitement. "Oh, Brendan. I love her already." She hooks her arm through Laura's. "So, which do you want to try first, sweetheart? My award-winning double-dark-chocolate coconut pie, the raspberry cream, or something more traditional, like pumpkin or apple?"

The women disappear into the house. I'm about to start up the walk after them, when Steve puts a hand on my shoulder again.

"Thanks for this, son. Angie's been over the moon since you called yesterday," he says, his gaze misty behind his wire-rimmed glasses. "I know it might feel strange to be here with someone other than Mary, but this is going to be good. For everyone. And it's what Mary would have wanted. As her dad, there's no doubt in my mind about that. From the time she was a tiny thing, she had the sweetest, most generous heart."

My throat goes tight, and a familiar wave of grief washes into my chest—soft, like the tide rolling in, not the tsunami of pain that used to hit, hard and without warning, in the early days after the accident, but still potent.

I still miss her.

I'm not sure I'm ready to move on, no matter what my in-laws, my friends, or my cock have to say about it. I care about Laura, and I want to fuck her with the desperation of a man who's been deprived of the comfort and release of sexual intimacy for over three years, but I'm not ready to fall in love again.

Make love, yes, but everything that goes with it—no. Hell no.

That certainty makes it easier to force a smile for Steve and say, "Thanks. I'm glad you guys are getting to meet Laura. She's something special."

And she is. She's sexy, fun, passionate, and great with kids, and I'm sure someday she'll make the right guy very happy. But that guy won't be me. She deserves to date someone whole and capable of making her dreams comes true, not a fractured man who might never fully recover from losing the woman he promised to love and cherish.

Promises like that aren't intended to be easily broken. Maybe for most people, death makes moving on easier, but that hasn't been the case for me.

SEXY MOTHERPUCKER

And I can't be anyone but who I am, no matter how many people—including myself—wish I were someone else.

CHAPTER Eight

Brendan

Inside the house, the smell of roasting turkey mingles with the fragrance of homemade bread, cookies, and rows of pies set out to cool on racks near the oven. The second I step through the door, my mouth starts to water, and by the time I've dropped Laura's suitcase and my bag in our room and unpacked Chloe's things in hers, my stomach is growling loud enough to be audible over the chatter in the kitchen.

"Oh, my. I heard that." Angie laughs as she turns away from the island, where Chloe and Laura are sitting bent over a book, in front of their already empty pie plates. "I'm guessing you're ready for pie now, too. Raspberry or coconut? I know you have no patience for pumpkin."

"I have patience for it, I just don't enjoy it," I

say, smiling as I see what Laura and Chloe are looking at. "Raspberry for me, please."

"Coming right up." Angie bustles over to the cabinet to grab a plate, while I circle around the pair of redheads bent over Chloe's baby book.

No matter how many times Chloe pages through the thing, she never gets tired of seeing pictures of herself as a baby. And honestly, neither do I.

"And this is when I had my first bath in the sink." Chloe grins up at Laura as she adds in a whisper, "Now you've seen me naked!"

Laura smiles. "That's okay. We're both girls. And you were just a baby."

"The prettiest baby," I add in a sappy voice, because I know it will bug Chloe.

On cue, she turns to poke me in the stomach and says, "Dad, stop!"

I grin. "But it's true. You were the prettiest baby I've ever seen. Though you looked nothing like your mom or me."

Chloe points to the next page and a picture of Maryanne laughing as baby Chloe splashes water on her T-shirt. "That's my mom. She had brown hair and Dad had blond when he was a baby. I take after Gammy."

"You do," Angie says proudly, sliding my pie across the island to the place at the empty stool next to Laura's.

"But you've got your daddy's eyes," Laura says, surprising me.

"Yep." Chloe leans forward, grinning at me, a wicked dimple popping in her cheek so I know the usual joke is coming. "Which is way better than his big old butt!"

Laura laughs as Angie shakes her head and clucks her tongue. "Oh, stop it. You're going to embarrass your dad."

Chloe wiggles happily on her stool, enjoying messing with me as much as she always does when she has an audience. "But he does have a big butt."

"His butt is perfectly proportionate to the rest of him," Laura says, defending me again, which is both endearing and embarrassing. Because we're talking about my butt in front of my daughter and my mother-in-law, and I'm not sure what it says about my parenting skills that I need defending from my seven-year-old.

"You're just being nice," Chloe says, giggling. "That butt is out there!"

"Okay, okay," I cut in as I reach for the whipped cream can. "Enough butt talk. Unless we're talking about the bare baby butt on the next page."

Chloe slaps a hand down on the book. "No way! I don't—"

She's cut off by a growl from Fluffster, Angie's West Highland terrier, as he bounds into the breakfast room behind us, deep in battle with the toy of the week. Around the Gibbons' house, toys rarely last longer than five or six days.

Fluffster is a dainty ball of white fluff—hence the name—but he goes into beast mode with his toys. I've seen more stuffed raccoons and giraffes ripped limb from limb than I can count.

I turn, expecting to see something stuffed and missing an eye or a leg, but I can't immediately peg what kind of toy he's got locked in his jaws this time. It takes me a moment to identify the nature of that floppy rubber disc, but by that time, Laura is already flying off her stool and lunging for the floor.

Angie's hand flies to cover her mouth as Laura begs in a strained tone, "Okay, puppy, give that back!"

She reaches for the diaphragm Fluffster must have liberated from the purse she left on the floor in our room—I should have warned her about the dog, dammit—but the little monster bounds away, clearly thinking it's playtime. He shakes his head, sending the contraceptive flopping dramatically.

"Fluffster, stop it right now," Angie orders firmly. "Put that down."

"Here, I'll help," Chloe says, spinning on her stool.

Before she can hop down, Angie, Laura, and I all shout, "No, Chloe!" in one jointly horrified voice.

But Laura is clearly the most mortified. Her face is flushed a pink so bright it looks like she let Chloe do her makeup again, and the horror in her voice as she crawls forward on all fours, cooing, "Come here, Fluffster. Come here boy. Come here and give me that toy," is enough to make me want to melt through the floor, and I'm not the kind who's easily embarrassed.

But then I've never had the dog drag one of my condoms out for show and tell in front of the family, either.

Finally, Laura manages to get hold of one end of the disc, but Fluffster isn't the kind of dog who gives up without a fight. The battle for the birth control goes on for another endless minute, as Chloe repeatedly asks "What is that?" in a high-pitched voice, Angie covers her mouth with both hands, and I try to figure out what would be the best way to help Laura—getting down on the floor to aid in the fight, or staying where I am so she's the only one with her hands on her...*ahem*...very personal property.

Before I can make a final call, Laura tugs the diaphragm from the dog's mouth and stands up, breath rushing out as she holds it over her head, out of reach of the dog who is leaping up and down, clearly determined to get his teeth back on the toy and keep the good times rolling.

"Okay, so that happened." She glances around the room, carefully avoiding making eye contact. "I'll just dispose of this, dig a hole, and hide there for a few thousand years. Be right back."

I stand with my napkin in hand, ready to help conceal the evidence of Fluffster's crime, but before I can cross the room, Laura makes a break for the sliding glass door leading to the patio and the backyard beyond. She slips swiftly out through a gap and closes it just as quickly, trapping an unhappy Fluffster inside the house as he tries to follow.

I turn back to Angie, but before I can ask her to keep Chloe inside, she waves in a shooing motion "Go! Let her know there's no reason to be embarrassed. Chloe and I will stay here and get the salad ready for later."

"Why should she be embarrassed?" I hear Chloe ask as I hurry for the door.

Angie assures her, "No reason at all, sweet pea. Now hop down and get me the carrots and the celery from the fridge. If we hurry you can chop a few before your daddy gets back and takes the knives away."

I'm not a fan of Chloe and knives, but I'm so grateful to Angie that I don't stop to remind Chloe of how she almost hacked off her finger helping chop walnuts last Christmas. I hurry out into the backyard, grateful for the thermal shirt under my sweater. It's a good twenty degrees colder here than in the city, and they've already seen substantial snowfall this season.

Snowfall that thankfully makes it easy to follow the Laura-boot-shaped imprints in the field of white blanketing the ground...

The prints track around the swing set to the back gate, where they disappear. I let myself out of the yard and start down the path leading away from the house, growing increasingly concerned as Laura's trail continues deeper and deeper into the woods.

I call her name, my voice echoing through the bare trees. "Laura, come back! It's okay. Chloe's been distracted, and Angie doesn't care. Neither do I."

"Well, I care." The muffled words come from the ground just ahead.

I round the curve and see Laura sitting on a fallen tree trunk, digging at the earth between her boots with a stick, the mangled diaphragm lying in the snow not far away.

I crouch down, sitting on my heels on the other side of the hole she's made. "You know they have trashcans back at the house."

"I'm going to bury it." She sniffs and swipes the back of her hand across her nose, her attention trained on the soil she's turning over one stick-stab at a time. "I'm going to bury it, and then I'm going to dig another hole for me."

I tilt my head, getting my first good view of her pink cheeks and the damp trails leading from her eyes down to the curve of her jaw. "Seriously, Freckles," I say gently. "There's no need to cry. I promise. It's not a big deal."

"It *is* a big deal." She sniffs harder. "And I'm not crying. Like I said last summer, I don't cry."

"And like I said, I don't think that's healthy." I brush her hair over her shoulder as I shift to sit on the log beside her. "It's okay to cry. But you don't need to cry about this. Honestly. It's just one of those things that happen when you have kids or dogs. Or kids *and* dogs. That's an especially dangerous combination."

But she isn't in the mood to laugh about this yet.

She shakes her head, sending the curtain of silky red slipping back between us. "I should have taken it out of my purse. I don't know why I left it in. It's not like I was expecting…"

She trails off, leaving me to fill in the blanks.

I clear my throat. "Yeah, well, best to be prepared, right? Just in case. Things have happened before."

She goes still, but I can feel her attention shifting my way behind the hair concealing most of her face.

"I brought condoms," I confess, hoping it will make things better, not worse. It's hard to know, but surely realizing she's not the only one who believes in being responsible and prepared will take the edge off of the shame she's feeling.

After a beat, she turns, staring at me with an inscrutable expression. "Why did you do that?"

"Because I'm attracted to you," I say, the confession alone enough to make me thicker. "And even though I know we're just friends…"

Her eyes darken as she echoes, "Even though you know we're just friends…"

"I still want to do this." I lean closer, slowly

threading my fingers into her hair, giving her ample opportunity to tell me to fuck off.

But she doesn't. She lets me get closer, closer, until her mouth is warm against mine and hunger dumps into my bloodstream, making my pulse race. Our lips brush softly, once, twice, a boundary-testing kiss that picks up steam as her lips part, offering me an invitation I can't refuse.

With a groan, I swirl my tongue against hers and into the sweetness of her mouth. She tastes like raspberry pie and whipped cream, but beneath that is sea spray, ocean breeze, and sun-warmed skin, making me wonder if she tastes like summer all year long. It can't be more than twenty-five or thirty degrees out here, but suddenly I'm back on the beach, burning all over because this woman is in my arms, bringing me into the light with her kiss.

CHAPTER Nine

Laura

I should stand up. Pull away. Run from this man as fast as my kiss-weakened knees can carry me.

This *isn't* what I want.

I'm not in the market for stolen kisses on the rare occasions when Brendan forgets how poorly he believes I would fit into his "complicated life." I'm not up for being fuck buddies or friends with benefits. I don't want to get off and pretend it doesn't mean more than that. That *he* doesn't mean more. That he doesn't make me ache for reasons that have nothing to do with how much I enjoy being in bed with him.

But as Brendan threads his fingers into my hair, fusing our mouths tight, every stroke of his tongue sending longing burning across my skin to pool hot and heavy between my thighs, I can't seem to force my hands to push him away.

Instead, when he lifts me, guiding my knees to either side of his hips until I'm straddling him on the fallen tree, all I do is gasp and press closer. Press my mouth closer to his lips and my breasts closer to his chest, while my hips roll forward, rocking against the thick ridge of his cock through our jeans.

"God, you feel so good," he murmurs, his hand finding its way up the front of my sweater. His fingers are cold against my tight nipple, but my skin is so warm I barely notice.

I left my coat inside, but I'm not the least bit chilly. I'm burning with the need to get closer to Brendan, to feel him heavy on top of me and thick between my thighs, driving me so out of my mind with pleasure that I forget what a stupid idea it is to touch him like this again.

"You're so fucking beautiful. I want you so much." He rolls my nipple back and forth between his calloused fingertips until it feels like electricity is shooting directly from his fingers to sizzle between my legs. "I really wish we had an un-mangled diaphragm with us right now."

The words help slam on the brakes, bringing me back from the brink of insanity before it's too late.

"We're not having sex in your in-laws' backyard," I say, pushing his hand from my breast.

His fingers mold to my ribs, clearly not ready

to beat a full retreat just yet. "Technically we're in the woods *behind* my in-laws' backyard."

"Or there, either." I tap his forearm, but his hand doesn't move. "Or anywhere else. We're *friends*, Brendan."

"I know. And I like being your friend." His eyes darken as he adds in a huskier voice, "But I also like making you feel good. The entire drive up here, all I could think about was how sweet you taste, and how much I love making you come on my mouth."

I shake my head, keeping my gaze fixed on his sweater, hoping he can't see the pain I'm sure is filling my eyes as he makes it crystal clear that all he wants from me is friendship with sex on the side. "No." I stand, detangling myself from him as gracefully as possible as I straddle-walk backward in the snow until I've cleared his knees. "That's not what I want."

"All right," he says, sounding disappointed. But then, men often experience disappointment when they've worked up a hard-on that isn't going to be put to use. It doesn't mean he's emotionally invested. "Friends, then?"

I nod. "I think that's for the best. For everyone."

He sighs. "That's what Steve said when we were walking into the house. That bringing you here was the best decision for everyone, no matter how strange it might feel." He runs a clawed hand through his hair with a bitter laugh.

"Must be nice to be so sure about things. I can't remember the last time I made a decision without second-guessing myself five or six fucking times."

"Well, I'm sure it's harder for you." I cross my arms below my still aching breasts, which aren't any happier about being away from Brendan than the rest of me. "You've got two people's lives and futures to consider."

He glances up, pain flashing in his eyes. "You cut me too much slack, Freckles."

"No, I don't. I cut you just enough," I say, before adding in a firmer voice, "But I don't want to go here again, okay? This is the last time we blur the lines."

Because I don't know if I'll be strong enough to tell you no next time.

And I can't let myself make love to a man who only wants to get off, or I'll regret it every night I cry myself to sleep wondering why you don't feel for me the things I feel for you.

I keep my weak thoughts to myself, forcing my expression to remain calmly neutral as Brendan tucks his chin to his chest. "Got it. I'm sorry I made things more awkward than they have to be. I didn't mean to. I just… I guess I don't know how to do this anymore. With anyone."

I nod, his words offering comfort. At least a little bit. "It's okay."

"No, it's not. But thank you. For everything. I appreciate what you're doing for Chloe and me, and I promise I won't forget where we stand again."

"Well, on the bright side, it took my mind off wrestling the dog for my diaphragm in front of Angie and Chloe." With the tip of my boot I toe the mangled rubber cup into the hole I dug and scuff earth on top of it. "Guess we should head back in and face the music."

He stands. "There's no music to face. Angie is one of the coolest people I've ever met. By the time we go in, she'll have distracted Chloe and it will be like it never happened."

I grimace as I back toward the trail. "I seriously doubt that."

"Just wait and see." He moves around me, taking care not to brush any part of me with any part of him, making every hormone in my body sob in despair.

Because hormones don't care about what's best for your heart or your head. Hormones just want to throw themselves on the sex fire and roll around in the coals until you've got third-degree burns.

I trail Brendan down the path and through the gate leading into the backyard, careful to keep a safe distance. By the time we slip back through the sliding door into the kitchen, Chloe is standing on a stepladder chopping carrots on a cutting board, while piano music plays from speakers arranged on top of the cabinets.

As we cross to the stools we vacated earlier, she looks up, dropping the knife and lifting her hands into the air, fingers spread wide in surrender. "Gammy told me I could keep cutting while she went to get something in her room. I promise, she did. You can ask her when she gets back."

"I did indeed." Angie, a paper bag in hand, breezes back into the room before Brendan can respond. "Chloe is doing a great job and being very careful. I think she might be a chef when she grows up."

"Or maybe when I'm ten." Chloe beams as she reclaims her knife. "They have cooking shows for kids now, Gammy. And they do all the cutting and put things in the oven by themselves and everything."

"I don't think you're quite ready to put things in the oven, but this looks good." Brendan circles around the island to survey Chloe's work as Angie puts a gentle arm around my shoulder, drawing me to the far corner of the room.

Inwardly, I'm cringing, but I plaster a smile on my face, determined to apologize and put the GDD—Great Diaphragm Debacle—behind us as quickly as possible. But before I can speak, Angie shakes her head and wags a warning finger.

"Don't worry about a thing." Her voice is pitched low, making it clear this moment is between us girls. "I just wanted to give you this, and we won't say another word about it. Though, I would like to apologize for my naughty dog. Fluffster has a knack for finding things he shouldn't." She presses the bag into my hand with a wink, before turning with a clap of her hands. "Okay, celery next, Chef Chloe. I want to see how skinny you can get the slices."

The doorbell rings, and Brendan heads for the front of the house. "I'll get that. It's probably Diana. She said she would be here around eleven."

He disappears through the doorway leading into the living room as I open the bag and peek inside to discover strips of…condoms. Strips and strips, enough for Brendan and me to get it on in every room in this house and still have a few dozen left over. My jaw drops and my cheeks flush what I'm certain is a shocking shade of red.

I'm still standing in the corner, wondering how I'm ever going to make eye contact with Angie again, when a petite woman with dark blond curls appears in front of me.

"Hi, I'm Diana, Brendan's sister. You must be Laura. It's so great to meet you." She lunges forward, pulling me into a one-armed hug as she adds in a softer voice, "Sounds like you need an escape. Stay close. I'll have us out on a long, head-clearing walk before you can say 'Fluffster is an asshole.'"

My breath rushes out in a relieved laugh. "Sounds good."

She pulls back with a wink. "No problem. I've got your back, sister." She holds up a canvas bag filled with wine bottles. "And I've got goodies for later. Soon we will be drunk, full of good food, and feeling no pain."

I give her a thumbs-up, scurry upstairs to hide my lunch bag full of condoms deep in the bowels of my suitcase, grab my coat, and return to the kitchen in time for Chloe to grab my hand on her way to the garage. "Come on, Laura. Come watch me ride my bike with Aunt Dee!"

"Can't wait." With one last glance into the kitchen—where Brendan is helping Angie fetch oversize platters from the uppermost cabinet shelves—I make my escape.

CHAPTER Ten

Laura

Outside in the cool air—which is much more pleasant now that I've rescued my coat from my luggage and added a matching scarf to go with my hat—I cup my hands around my mouth and shout down the mostly deserted street, "Don't get too far ahead, Chloe!"

Chloe waves a hand in response and veers into a cul-de-sac, where she seems content to guide her bike in circles until Diana and I catch up.

"She'll be fine," Diana says. "Chloe's solid on her bike, and most of the people in the neighborhood go to visit family for the holidays. It's always weirdly deserted around here at American Thanksgiving."

"American Thanksgiving? As opposed to…" I smile down at my petite savior. It's hard to believe Diana and Brendan are related by blood.

She's as delicate as he is tall and broad, with soft brown eyes in contrast to his piercing blue. The only thing they have in common is their dark blond curls, which Diana has twisted up into an artistic knot atop her head, secured by a number two pencil.

"As opposed to Canadian Thanksgiving," she says. "The true and original Thanksgiving, first celebrated in Newfoundland by Sir Martin Frobisher and his crew in 1578, a good forty-something years before the Pilgrims." She grins as she lifts the camera dangling around her neck and snaps a picture of me, moving so quickly I don't have time to smile. "Don't worry; you look gorgeous in this light. It's going to be a great shot. I'll send it to Brendan when I get the film developed. I know no one does film anymore, but I get sentimental around the holidays. Even American holidays. Brendan did mention that he's Canadian, didn't he?"

I nod, wishing I'd had another cup of coffee. Diana's an even faster talker than I am. "Yeah. I knew he grew up on Vancouver Island, but he never mentioned Canadian Thanksgiving. Maybe he assumed I knew. I should have, I guess. I've lived one state away from the border my entire life."

"It's okay. You know Canadians; we don't like to brag about our superior holiday celebrations." She grins. "And it's not a huge deal in our family. Our parents usually host something low key at their place in October, and then Brendan and I come here for the gluttonous American version in November. The Gibbons were nice enough to adopt me along with Brendan when he and Maryanne got married, so I'm a regular by this point."

"They do seem very nice," I say, my cheeks heating all over again.

Diana laughs. "They really are. And seriously, the embarrassing stuff will be old news by the time we sit down for dinner. Angie always underestimates how long it's going to take for the turkey to cook. We'll be lucky to be eating before five. By then everyone will be so starved they won't care about anything except shoveling food into their mouths as quickly as humanly possible."

"Good to know." I cross my arms at my chest with a sigh. "Though, I doubt I'll be able to look Angie in the eye without blushing for quite some time. It's going to be a long weekend."

Diana rests a hand on my arm, pulling me to a gentle stop beside her, her expression sobering. "Hey, before we get close enough for Chloe to hear, I want you to know that I know. Brendan told me about the favor you're doing for him. He really appreciates it, and so do I. The Gibbons are amazing people, but they're also kind of crazy when it comes to Chloe's happiness. I don't *think* they would try to fight Brendan for custody—at least not as long as he keeps holding it together as well as he has been—but it's not completely out of the realm of possibility, and I know it's been freaking him out. Having you here will go a long way to getting them off his back."

She shrugs, her eyes narrowing as her smile widens, making her resemble a cat preparing to pounce a mouse stuffed with catnip. "And who knows? It might be the kick in the ass you guys need to realize reality is more fun than pretend. Because let's get real—you have a thing for my brother, don't you?"

"Um…" I press my lips together, casting a furtive glance Chloe's way. But Chloe is still peddling in happy circles, singing a song from one of her favorite cartoons, oblivious that I'm being questioned by a master of interrogation disguised as a cute blond woman.

"It's cool," Diana hurries on. "If he hasn't caught on yet, I won't say anything. But so you know, my brother is one of the good ones. I'm of the opinion that men, as a whole, aren't worth the trouble, but he's an exception. He's a solid, generous, decent guy. And he can be fun, too, if you can get him to relax."

I tuck my chin to my chest, studying the cracked sidewalk, wishing I'd stayed inside. Yes, I'd felt about two seconds away from spontaneously combusting from embarrassment, but at least I could have avoided yet another awkward conversation. "Yeah. I saw that side this past summer. We had a lot of fun together for a little while, but he…"

I take a deep breath, forcing a smile as I look up, meeting Diana's searching gaze. "But that's all he was up for. He's not interested in feelings, and I'm not interested in the other stuff without feelings, so…"

A frown wrinkles Diana's delicate brow. "Oh, shit. I'm sorry. I had no idea. He never said anything, and the way he was looking at you when we walked into the kitchen, I assumed…" Her nose wrinkles as she brings the heel of her palm to smack her forehead. "Now I feel like a complete ass. I'm so sorry."

"It's okay." I wave a hand through the air between us. "There's no way you could have known."

"No, seriously, I have the worst luck with relationships. I know nothing about the finding, let alone the care and feeding, of love. I should have learned to keep my mouth shut years ago." She lunges forward, giving me another hug, this time a two-armed version, smashing her camera painfully between us. "I'm sorry I made things uncomfortable, and I'm sorry my brother's a fuckhead."

I laugh, patting her on the back. "He's not a fuckhead."

"No, he is," she says earnestly as she pulls away. "He told you all he wanted was a fuck buddy, and then asked you to come pretend to be his girlfriend? That's the definition of a fuckhead."

"It's more complicated than that. And I don't think he has any idea I have feelings for him. We went back to being friends after. If anything, he's clueless, not cruel."

She props her hands low on her hips. "Being clueless is no excuse. He needs to get that memo, and I'm going to make sure he does, loud and clear. I won't tolerate my brother becoming one of the useless dicks of the world. He was raised better."

I hold up my hands, shaking my head fast. "Oh, please don't. Don't say anything to him. I've already had enough embarrassment to last me for the next several years. Let me cling to what pride I have left."

Diana sighs, her arms falling listlessly to her sides. "All right. But be sure to give me your address before I leave tonight, okay? That way I can send copies of the good pics straight to you. Brendan doesn't deserve beautiful candid shots of the gorgeous woman he's too stupid to fall madly in love with."

My lips curve. "You're very sweet. But in his defense, I'm not going to take the rejection personally anymore. After a few of the things he said today, I don't think Brendan is ready to give anyone a chance. It's not just me."

"I think you're right." Diana fiddles with one of the knobs on top of her camera. "It's hard enough to move on after a relationship ends in a bad breakup. I can't imagine how hard it must be for him. Still...I wish he could find a way to open up again. It's hard to see someone you love living life at fifty percent, you know?" Her gaze goes wistful and her fingers still. "My brother's like a unicorn with his horn cut off. Still mostly whole and functional, but the magic is gone."

I'm not sure how to respond to that odd, yet sadly accurate, comparison, but thankfully Chloe saves me.

"Are you two coming or not?" she calls out from the end of the block. "We're never going to get to the waterfall if you don't keep walking."

"Coming, Miss Bossy." Diana's eyes flash as she nods toward her niece. "But that one's pretty magical, huh? Almost makes me want to consider artificial insemination."

I grin as I fall back into step beside her. "Agreed. Though I do enjoy borrowing other people's kids. My sister's in a pretty intense relationship. I have a suspicion I'll be an aunt before too long."

"Being an aunt is the best!" Diana lifts her camera, snapping a picture of Chloe as she peddles down the street, her hair flying in the breeze. "All the fun of being a mom, and then you can ghost when the fairy child starts showing her demon side. So, you just have one sister?"

"Just one. But Libby's boyfriend and I have been tight since we were kids, so he kind of feels like a brother already. Is Brendan your only brother?"

She nods. "Yep, it's all girls in the Daniels' house except him. But my other sisters are still on the island, so they don't pester him as much as I do."

The rest of the way to the waterfall, we talk about families—the pluses and minuses of a large tribe over a small one—work, travel, and other safe subjects. Diana pulls out her phone, showing me some of her favorite shots from her years as a wildlife photographer for the National Park System, and I tell her about the hockey fantasy camp I organize for the Badgers every February.

At the waterfall, which is only partially frozen, but entirely stunning, Chloe gives me a tour, while Diana snaps pictures. Afterward, we leave Chloe's bike leaned against the guardrail and hike up into the woods behind the falls, climbing until we're treated with truly stunning views of the gorge and snow-covered Mount Hood beyond.

Nature works its usual magic, and by the time we get back down to street level, I'm feeling more at peace than I did before. Hiking through the dramatic scenery of the Pacific Northwest, it's hard not to feel like life is simpler than I usually give it credit for. My problems have been put in perspective by the epic mountain range stretching toward the horizon, evergreens towering overhead, and sunlight glittering on snow.

So I've got a thing for a man who doesn't have a thing for me—who clearly wants me but doesn't want the messy possibilities that come along with getting emotionally involved with another human being. Compared to the settlers who made their way across the mountains in covered wagons, starving and struggling and fighting their way to a new life, my problems are pretty fucking small.

My zen state lasts the entire walk back to the house, through several hours in Chloe's room watching movies and building an obstacle course of Legos for Fluffster—who has decided he loves me and would prefer not to be parted from my side, proving there is no bond as powerful as that between a woman and a dog who've done battle over a diaphragm—and throughout dinner, which is even later than Diana predicted.

We sit down at six, our company joined by Angie's sister and her three adult children, seven of Chloe's second cousins between the ages of four and fifteen, and an elderly couple from down the street who have no relatives in the area. We finish our second serving of pie at eight fifteen, just in time for Chloe to be whisked away to her room, her sleepy arms wrapped around her daddy's neck and her head resting on his shoulder. I help clear the table and tidy up the kitchen as the guests bundle into their coats, I hug Diana at the door, and finally I bid Angie and Steve good night around nine.

It isn't until I'm trudging up the stairs, tired from a long day of kisses, embarrassment, more kisses, mortification, hiking, playing, and eating too much pie that I start to feel anxious again.

Since I returned from the walk, Brendan and I haven't had much time to play the happy couple. He was busy helping Steve set up extra folding tables in the living room and fixing something plumbing related in the guest bathroom, and I was busy entertaining Chloe and helping Angie serve the kids.

Now, as I slip into our shared room to hear water running in the attached bathroom, the reality that Brendan and I are going to be sharing the queen bed against the far wall makes my mouth dry and my heart beat faster. After this morning, I know nothing's going to happen between us, but that doesn't mean I won't spend the entire night lying awake, very, *very* aware of the warm, powerful, beautiful body of the man sleeping next to me.

I'm debating telling Brendan that I'll sleep in the Cruiser and sneak back into our room before sunrise tomorrow to maintain our cover—sure, I might freeze as the temperature drops overnight, but at least I'll be able to get some sleep before I die of hypothermia—when he sticks his head out of the bathroom, a damp washcloth in hand.

"Hey. I was just headed downstairs to say goodbye to Diana."

"She already left." I unzip my suitcase, which Brendan has relocated to the bench at the foot of the bed, giving me the prime luggage space while leaving his own on the floor.

"She did?" He frowns, stepping through the door. "You're sure?"

I nod, concentrating on pulling out my sleep things—the most modest pair of flannel pajamas I own—to avoid admiring how good Brendan looks in black sweatpants and a tight blue T-shirt. We slept naked the last time we spent the night together. I've never seen him dressed for bed, and he looks unexpectedly…snuggly.

Sexy and snuggly, a dangerous combination.

He curses softly. "Great. She must be pissed at me for some reason."

I shrug. "Maybe she was just tired. She has a long drive, right?"

"A couple of hours. She's based out of Crater Lake right now, but she's staying with a friend in Eugene tonight. I'll text her in the morning and see what's up." He sighs tiredly, flipping the washcloth over his shoulder. "I'm not in the mood for a Diana fight tonight." He glances up, his eyes guarded. "So, I think it went okay, don't you?"

"I think it went very well." I smile. "After the initial insanity."

His lips curve. "You made an excellent recovery."

"Well, I'm made of pretty tough stuff." I turn to face him, my pajamas held to my chest. "Is it okay if I grab a shower before bed?"

"Sure. I'm done. It's all yours." He steps aside,

motioning to the tub with an awkwardness that would be endearing if I didn't know the reason for it.

"It's cool," I say with forced levity, knowing I can't survive another three days of "sorry about trying to get into your pants" Brendan. "We're cool. Let's forget about everything that happened between ten and eleven a.m. and move on with a fresh slate, okay?"

He nods, but the tension around his eyes remains. "Okay. But I'm going to sleep on the floor."

"You don't have to do that," I say, though the thought of a few extra feet between sleeping Brendan and sleeping me actually sounds like a good idea.

"No, it's fine. I'll grab an extra blanket out of Chloe's room and be fine on the floor." He backs toward the door, jabbing a thumb over his shoulder. "I can sleep anywhere. I'll probably be out cold before you get out of the shower. I know it's early, but I'm pretty beat."

"Me, too." I flutter my fingers. "Good night, then."

"Good night." He pauses in the doorway, his lips parting, but after a moment he shakes his head and lifts a hand, clearly rethinking whatever he was going to say. "See you in the morning."

And then he's gone, and there is suddenly more oxygen in the room. Which is good. Oxygen is good. Breathing is good.

SEXY MOTHERPUCKER

So why does watching him go feel so shitty?

CHAPTER Eleven

Brendan

After another rough night, spent listening to Laura moan softly in her sleep and wishing I was next to her, with my arms wrapped around her and her fine ass tucked against me, the last thing I want to do is get up at the crack of dawn and rush up the mountain.

But Chloe is up at six fifteen, knocking on the bedroom door, asking if I packed her unicorn ski pants and if she can have pancakes *and* pie for breakfast and how much longer until we leave. By the time I locate the pants—and the matching unicorn hat that Justin made for her—and stumble downstairs for coffee, Steve and Angie are already dressed in their ski clothes and looking way too bright-eyed for people who fed a small army yesterday and helped take down five bottles of wine last night.

"Ready to hit the slopes, killer?" Steve asks. "I've been missing my black diamond buddies. Angie won't do the big runs with me anymore."

I give him two sleepy thumbs-up, and add extra sugar to my coffee.

I'm tired now, but by the time I'm on a lift, the crisp air at seven thousand feet will wake me up. Chloe and I have both been looking forward to this weekend. I grew up spending Christmas holidays with my grandparents in Banff, skiing from sunup to sundown, and she's been skiing like a champ since she was four years old.

By nine o'clock, we're dressed for the elements and the Cruiser is packed with a cooler filled with turkey sandwiches and drinks, two bags of snacks to keep our energy up through early evening, and Chloe's skis. Steve and Angie lead the way in their truck, heading out of the subdivision and onto the highway toward the Government Camp ski area.

"So why don't you have your own skis?" Laura asks. She's sitting up front with me today, looking like a Viking princess in her tight red ski pants and black and white snowflake sweater, making me glad she's planning to stick to the blue runs with Angie today. I'm not sure how I would hold up to an entire day of exposure to her ass in those pants.

"I don't know." I shrug, fighting to keep my eyes on the road and my thoughts in the friend zone. She made her position on being more than that perfectly clear yesterday. Continuing to dwell on how much I wish I hadn't fucked up my chance with her is only going to make the weekend pass even more slowly. "When I first moved here to play for the Badgers I wasn't sure I would have time to ski. And then there were a few years, when Chloe was a baby, when I didn't make it up to the slopes the entire season."

"But now I ski better than Dad," Chloe pipes up from behind me. "Don't I, Dad?"

"You're very good." I catch her gaze in the rearview mirror. "But don't get cocky, okay? I want you to stick to the green and blue runs until after lunch. Give yourself a chance to get comfortable on your skis again."

"I'm already comfortable on my skis."

"Chloe," I say, her name a warning. "I'm serious. You haven't been out since last March. Stick to the green and blue until after lunch, or you're going to lose drawing time next week."

She grumbles something stubborn beneath her breath, but I feel fairly confident she's going to listen. I don't whip out threats to take away drawing time unless I mean business.

"That's funny," Laura says softly after Chloe returns to the picture she's coloring. "For most kids, it would be dessert or video games or something."

"But that's not what she loves most. The only way I ever get her to listen is to hit her where it hurts."

Laura nods, studying me from the corner of her eye.

"What?" I finally ask.

"You're a good dad. You've got a good mix of discipline and affection going on. She knows she's loved, but she also has boundaries. It's…good."

I adjust my grip on the steering wheel, flustered by the compliment. "Thanks. I try my best."

"That's obvious." She takes a sip of her coffee and reaches out to adjust her heat vent. "It's also obvious that Chloe's a lot happier on days with no school in them."

"Aren't we all? I mean, I love my job, but I'm still more fun on the weekend."

"I'll take your word for it," she says, softening the words with a smile. "I know I already mentioned this, but it might not be such a bad thing for Chloe to go back to her old school. Maybe at least give it a try. And then if she's still struggling, you'll know it's adjusting to first grade that's the problem, not the learning environment at Elmwood." She lifts her coffee cup between us. "And that advice is coming from my sister, by the way, who is a real-life elementary school teacher. A very good one, who wins awards and inspires undying devotion in her students and stuff. So…"

I nod, the conversation hitting me differently than it did the last time Laura brought it up. Of course, that was almost six weeks ago, before I realized how much she cares about Chloe.

"I'll think about it." I glance into the rearview mirror, grateful to see Chloe's head still bent over her coloring book. I don't want her to start thinking this is a done deal. "The year at Elmwood is already paid for. So maybe they would let her leave and come back if she needed to. And hopefully I'll have found a reliable nanny by Christmas so after school care won't be such a big deal." I shake my head, the familiar childcare-related stress creeping in to tighten my shoulders. "If not, I may have to fucking retire to make sure someone's always there to pick her up at school."

"I heard that! Another dollar in the swear jar for you when we get home," Chloe pipes up, making me cuss again beneath my breath.

Laura snorts. "You're right. She's always listening."

"Always," I agree, with a rueful smile.

"You'll find someone," Laura says. "You can't retire now, right when you're becoming one of my most cooperative Badger ambassadors."

"Forget that I'm captain and was voted MVP three years in a row. It's all about the PR."

"Yes!" She pats me on the thigh, making my cock twitch hopefully inside my boxers because the dumb bastard has the IQ of a single celled organism and hasn't caught on to the fact that Laura isn't ever going to be in our bed again. "Glad you're starting to understand that. Without

PR, those crowds watching you be MVP would be a lot smaller, my friend."

Her friend.

There are far worse things to be—Laura's a good friend, who is always there to help out with Chloe no matter how weird things are between us at any given moment—but the reminder makes me grumpy.

I pass the rest of the drive up to the ski area in silence, while Laura and Chloe discuss the merits of turkey sandwiches with mayo versus cranberry sauce, where the best blue runs are at the resort, and whether Chloe's unicorn hat is going to fit beneath her ski helmet.

"The horn is squishy, so I think it will." Chloe's legs kick faster as we pay the daily parking fee and pull into the already packed lot. "It's made of yarn and yarn squishes. That's a fact."

"Can't argue with facts." Laura glances over her shoulder, a warmth in her gaze that makes me feel even worse. My shitty judgment call last summer didn't just rob me of a gorgeous, sexy woman in my bed; it robbed Chloe of the female influence Steve and Angie want for her.

Yes, Chloe still sees a lot of Laura, but she would see more of her if we were dating.

And then when you broke up, she would see a lot less of her.

Better to maintain the status quo.

Four years ago, a thought like that never would

have crossed my mind. I was all about pushing my boundaries, bending the rules, and seeing how much extraordinary I could fit into one lifetime. But somewhere along the line, between the nightmarish day I received that call from the police, and the tolerable present, I stopped aiming for extraordinary. I became satisfied with an absence of pain and stopped hoping for pleasure. I became resigned to the status quo.

But right now, the status fucking quo feels like a rope binding my hands, keeping me from reaching for something better than good enough, and chafing like hell in the process.

"Can you carry your skis?" Laura asks Chloe, hooking one bulging snack bag over each shoulder. "If so, I think we can make it in one trip."

"I can carry my skis and my boots." Chloe prances back and forth in the fresh snow. "I'm so excited! I can't wait to go fast!"

"Not too fast," I say, because that's what stick in the mud, status-quo-loving, boring dads like me say. Even though I lived to go fast when I was Chloe's age, and no amount of grownup nagging ever slowed me down.

I am well aware that I'm flopping my lips in vain, but I flop them anyway because once fear has penetrated as deep into a person's marrow as it has into mine, logic has no power. My only victory against the cold, clutching, constricting emotion has been the fact that I continue to let

Chloe out of the house every day. I allow her to play and explore and do potentially dangerous things like ski, swim in the ocean, and go rock climbing with her grandparents every summer, even though the fear monster insists I'm risking losing her the way I lost her mom.

"You okay?" Laura lays a hand on my shoulder.

"Great," I grunt, lifting the heavy cooler and hauling it up the hill to the rental chalet, grateful for the chance to use my brawn instead of my brain. Hopefully, a few black diamond runs will get the fucking angst out of my system, and I can enjoy the day without being a moody son of a bitch.

I drop the cooler and Chloe with Angie on the second floor, where she's claimed a table next to a couple of lockers, and follow Steve and Laura down to the ski rental. We secure performance skis for ourselves and lift passes for the group and are out on the bunny slope twenty minutes later, gliding through the fresh powder to the bottom of the hill and the tiny lift Chloe used to ride all day long when she was first learning a few years ago.

Now, the kid can barely stand to warm up on the bunny slope. After two runs, she's already whining, "Come on, Dad. Let's go! I want to go up to Stormin' Norman."

"We'll get there." I settle onto the lift chair beside her as it whisks us into the air, high enough to catch a sweet view of Mount Hood behind the main lodge. "But let's give Laura a little more time on the bunny slope, okay? She said it's been a couple years since she skied."

Chloe glances down at the slope, where Laura is making her way competently, but cautiously, down the bunny hill. "She's not as good as I thought she would be." She turns back to me, a serious expression on her face. "But that's okay. You don't have to be great at skiing to have fun, and I can stay on the blue runs with her if she needs company."

I nudge her shoulder with mine, pride filling my chest. "You're a good kid, kid. I love you."

She wrinkles her nose. "I love you, too. Even though you have a big butt."

She laughs and I roll my eyes—because I understand that it's no fun teasing me unless I pretend to be irritated by it. We hop off at the end of the lift and Chloe zips immediately down the hill, swishing back and forth with an ease and control that's incredible in a seven-year-old.

On impulse, I tug my phone out of my pocket to snap a picture to send to my parents, who are always complaining that I don't send enough Chloe updates to satisfy their grandparent needs, to see a missed call from my sister and an epic string of texts I somehow didn't hear come through on the way up the mountain.

Diana: Okay, I promised I wouldn't say anything

to you about this, but I can't help myself. Because I feel like you're making a mistake, big brother. And I think you're lying to yourself. And as someone who messed up her life by lying to herself for way too long, I really don't want the same thing to happen to you.
I saw you with Laura yesterday, and that wasn't pretend, dude. I've seen your commercials for the steak house. We both know you're not that good an actor.
You've got a thing for her, Brendan.
There are real feelings there.
How can I tell, you ask?
BECAUSE I'M YOUR SISTER AND I KNOW YOU AND I KNOW THE DOPEY SAD LOOK YOU GET WHEN YOU'RE CRUSHING ON SOMEONE. IT'S BEEN THE SAME SINCE SEVENTH GRADE!
You remember Alicia Anderson? And what a jerk she was after you brought that stuffed panda to school for her on Valentine's Day?

With a scowl, I tug off one glove and text back, *Yeah, I do. Thanks for the trip down memory lane and for the all-caps insult, but it doesn't matter what I do or don't feel.*

Laura isn't interested in more than pretend.
She wants to be friends. That's it.

Diana: You're crazy. She's totally into you. I know this for a fact.

I glance up, waving at Chloe, who is already at the bottom of the hill with Laura, jabbing a thumb toward the blue run that starts to the right of the bunny slope. "Go ahead, I'll catch up," I shout.

Before I can text Diana again, and educate her on how solidly Laura turned me down just yesterday, another text pops through.

Diana: I know because she told me. But don't you dare tell her that I told you.
I don't want her to think I can't be trusted, because I usually can. But this time the greater good is best served by breaking my promise and telling you to pull your head out of your butt and ask her out for real before it's too late.
Call me if you want to discuss further, but only if you're not going to yell at me.
Amanda and I stayed up until two a.m. last night drinking margaritas, playing cards, and convincing each other we're glad that we're single and go to bed alone on major holidays.
So I'm hung over and have a low tolerance for loud noises.
But I love you.
I just want you to be happy, okay?

I text back a quick—*Love you, too. And thank you. I'll call later*—and zip my phone into my coat pocket. A second later, I've got my glove on, my poles in hand, and I'm shushing away down the bunny slope onto the blue run, heading after Chloe and Laura.

I have no idea what I'm going to say to Laura when I catch up to them—probably nothing, because Chloe will be listening and this isn't a conversation to have in front of a nosy seven-year-old who already thinks Laura and I are dating—but knowing there's even a slim chance that I misunderstood her yesterday banishes the gray cloud that's been hovering over my head all morning.

Maybe it's not too late.

And maybe I'm more ready to start dating than I thought.

Yes, I will always miss Maryanne. For the rest of my life, there's no denying that. But if I never get to be with Laura again, I'll miss that, too. I'll miss it—and her—way more than a person should miss a good friend. It's already more than friendship between us, and I, for one, would like to stop pretending that our relationship is working the way it is now.

Fuck the status quo.

I want more than that from the sexy redhead swishing down the trail in front of me, and I'm ready to fight for another chance, to do whatever it takes to prove to her that I won't screw things up the second time around.

I'm calculating the odds of catching up to Steve and Angie before they reach the lift at the bottom of the run—decent, even though they headed out ten minutes ago, since Angie likes to stop and take in the scenery—and composing an argument to get Chloe to ride the lift with her grandparents, giving me five minutes alone with Laura, which will hopefully be enough for me to convince her we should sneak away this afternoon to talk some more, when a sudden movement draws my attention.

I glance up the mountain to see a snowboarder in neon-green pants racing down a black diamond run. He veers into the woods, mowing over a slim evergreen that snaps upright with a puff of snow once he's clear, making the flakes glitter in the morning sun. Leaning hard to one side, he slips around a tree big enough to have given him the concussion he's clearly looking for and drops several feet through the air onto the packed snow.

I tense, expecting to see the kid wipe out, but he manages to find a path through the trees, his board skimming faster and faster, heading for the intersection between the blue and black runs at roughly the speed of light. It only takes a moment for me to calculate the distance between Chloe and the out of control douchebag, but by the time I open my mouth to shout a warning, it's too late.

Chloe's name passes my lips at the same time the snowboarder smashes into the snow right in front of her.

With a squeal of surprise, she cuts hard to the left to avoid a head-on collision, and a second later, my daughter is gone, shooting down a black diamond run without so much as the chance to tighten her grip on her poles.

CHAPTER Twelve

Laura

It all happens so fast.

An asshole on a snowboard bursts out of the woods in front of Chloe, sending her skidding off the trail. Before I can recover from the shock, or shout at the jerk to slow the hell down, she's gone, careening away down an insanely steep run.

"Chloe!" My heart leaps into my throat and lodges there, making me feel like I'm being strangled by my panic.

And then I'm gone, pushing off the trail, heading after her. Because apparently, that's what happens when you see a small person you care about in trouble. You race after them first and realize you're in over your head after it's too late to call the ski patrol and get a professional on the case.

The first five seconds of my plummet through

time and space are enough to assure me that this run is indeed a black diamond. Or maybe a double black diamond or a blood and crossbones diamond or whatever symbol means a scary as fuck, nearly vertical, loaded with bumps and rocks death trap. Only Olympic athletes should set skis on this sucker, and I am dangerously out of my element.

Gritting my jaw, I wedge my skis hard as I bounce back and forth through the lumpy snow, trying to maintain a downhill speed of moderately-insane instead of certain-doom-dangerous. As I skid hard to the right, barely managing to avoid slamming into another skier swishing confidently down the trail in front of me, I desperately wish I'd spent more time on skis as a child and less on figure skates.

But it's too late now. I'll just have to pray that my advanced beginner skills will be enough to help me tail Chloe down this monster in one piece.

My only comfort is that she seems to be faring better than I am. Her body language—shoulders hunched and poles wobbling in the air behind her like tiny helicopter blades—makes it clear she isn't enjoying our plunge any more than I am, but she's holding her own against the big bad mountain.

Thank God. As long as she gets down okay, that's all that matters.

The thought zips through my head, followed

quickly by the realization that I truly love that little girl. This isn't friendly affection. This is *love*, so powerful and real that I don't care if I end up breaking bones between here and the base of the mountain, as long as my shattered body will somehow ensure Chloe doesn't have to suffer.

My throat tightens, my eyes sting, and my ribs contract so swiftly that my chest feels bruised.

This isn't the time for an emotional breakdown or breakthrough or whatever is happening to me, but I can't help myself. All at once, I understand with a visceral certainty how terrifying it must be to be a mother. Or to be Brendan, with his heart walking around outside his body in French braids and unicorn ski pants, spouting sass and taking risks, all while having no clue how precious she is.

Precious and horrifyingly vulnerable.

All it takes is one bad call, one wrong move, one stupid mistake, one snowboarder who isn't paying attention to the "trails merging, go slow" sign to put her in the kind of danger she might not be able to bounce back from.

"Please, please, please," I chant as Chloe skids wildly around a turn in the trail, making my pulse spike as she narrowly avoids a collision with a boulder poking out of the snow.

Please let her be okay.

Please let her pull this off.

Please let her be waiting for me at the bottom of the run with a mouth full of the curse words she learned from spending too much time around professional hockey players. Please let her be whole and safe and in the mood to let me hug her tight, because, man, am I going to need a hug by the time this is over.

I make the same harrowing turn, getting even closer to the super scary boulder than Chloe did. Close enough that a vivid image of bloody brains splattered over obsidian rock flits through my mind, making every muscle in my body clench in fear.

And that's what does me in.

I can feel it, the moment my tension contributes to my velocity and my velocity grows too great to allow my whip-tight, weary muscles to shift my skis in the opposite direction. As I shoot into the woods, I catch a glimpse of the end of the run, the lift churning in slow, steady circles, whisking conquering heroes back up the mountain, and Chloe skidding to a stop beside the other people shuffling into the lift line.

Thank God. She made it. She's okay.

Relief courses through me, followed swiftly by a mental "oh shit!" as I narrowly avoid crashing into a tree with a trunk the size of a small car. I cut right, then left again, fighting to slow down, but the next big scary tree is already rushing toward me, and there's no escape route that doesn't send me on a fresh path to destruction.

There are trees fucking everywhere.

You would think it was a forest or something, a smartass voice in my head pipes up, only to be drowned out a moment later by a screamier internal voice howling, *Stupid way to die! Stupid way to die! This is such a stupid way to die!*

Using every bit of strength left in my trembling quad muscles, I wedge like my life depends on it, since it might—I left my helmet in my locker, as we were allegedly sticking to the easy runs—and hurl myself to the left, dropping my poles and reaching for the ground with arms outstretched, praying I'll find something to hold onto beneath the snow.

The good news is that I slow down, skidding to a stop as one ski pops off my boot and the other thuds solidly into the trunk of the giant tree. The bad news is that pain flashes through my right knee, sending a sharp, stretching, burning, "not right" sensation shooting through the joint and up the inside of my thigh.

"Oh, ow." My eyes squeeze shut. "Ow, ow, ow…"

It hurts like a son of a bitch. I'm pretty sure I did something to my knee that will make further frolicking in the snow impossible, but I'm alive. I'm alive, and Chloe is safe, and no brains have been splattered.

My heart beat is slowing, sending out "we're all right, time to quit freaking out" signals to the rest of my traumatized organs, when something whumps onto the snow beside me. A puff of powder explodes into the air, and my pulse leaps into overdrive all over again.

I flinch as I glance over my shoulder, only to sag with relief when I see Brendan popping his skis off beside me.

I press a hand to my chest, where I swear I can feel my heart thudding through my ski jacket, sweater, and ribs. "Shit, you scared me."

"That makes two of us," he says, tossing his poles onto the snow before kneeling beside me. "Are you all right? No, don't move, let me get you out of that ski first."

"I'm okay, but I did something to my right knee." He reaches for the latch connecting the boot on my injured leg to the ski, and I tense, but he's so careful I barely feel a thing until I shift to sit up in the snow, putting pressure on the joint. "Ouch. Yeah. Something's not right. I think I pulled a muscle or maybe a ligament or something."

Brendan's fingers prod the outside of my knee without causing any fresh pain, but when they move to the inside my shoulders shoot toward my ears and a whimper escapes through my clenched jaw.

He backs off fast. "I don't think it's your ACL. Could be the MCL, which is still bad, but it'll be easier to recover without reinjuring it. And nothing feels broken." His big hands circle my thigh, squeezing gently as his gaze meets mine, relief clear in his eyes. "You're lucky it's not worse. When I saw you shoot into the woods like that…"

He shakes his head as he brushes the snow from my jacket. "I thought I was going to have a heart attack. You shouldn't have gone after her, Laura. You could have gotten yourself killed."

"I couldn't help it," I whisper. "I saw her go off the trail and I just…went after her. I didn't even think. I was just so scared."

"I know." He tugs his glove off, skimming his hand over my hair, sending more snow falling to the ground and making me wonder at what point I lost my pom-pom hat. "Thank you."

"For what?" I sniff. "I didn't do anything."

"You risked your life trying to help my daughter. That's a pretty big deal in my book."

I blink, my vision swimming. "Yeah, well, I love her, stupid."

His eyes soften. "I am stupid. I'm sorry."

I lift a shoulder and let it fall with a laugh even as my throat gets tighter. "It's okay. We're all stupid sometimes."

"Some more than others." He leans closer, until I'm pretty sure he's about to kiss me again. But I decide I'm okay with that, since kisses, hugs, and all other forms of comfort are sounding good in the wake of my near-death experience—fuck it, I'll worry about redrawing my line in the sand once I'm not on the verge of going into shock—when a siren whoops behind him.

Brendan glances over his shoulder, lifting a hand to someone I can't see from my position flat on my butt in the snow. "Hey! We're over here! She's okay, but there's no way she's walking or skiing out. She tweaked something in her knee."

"Got it," a male voice says behind him. "We'll be there with a stretcher in a minute. You two hold tight."

Brendan turns back to me, relief and regret warring in his expression. "I should get down to the bottom and help Chloe. She made it to the lift line okay, but she'll be scared if one of us doesn't show up soon."

I nod, making shooing motions with my gloved hands. "Go. Tell her I'm fine, and I'll see you guys back at the chalet or wherever they take broken people."

"I'll call Angie and Steve, and we'll all meet you in the infirmary." He stands, but before he leaves, he bends low, pressing a kiss to my forehead. "I'm so glad you're all right."

And then he's gone, leaving me swimming in a strange mixture of melancholy and exhaustion, proving my adrenaline rush has truly left the building. Thankfully, the two ski patrol officers who arrive a moment later are sweet, adorable, hippie boys, clearly devoted to easing the pain and suffering of the recently wiped out.

They crack jokes and praise my not-running-into-trees-skills as they load me onto the stretcher like precious cargo and carry me through the woods to their snowmobile. They strap the stretcher, with me still laid out on top, onto the back of their ride and fire up the engine. The cutie with the brown beard drives, while the cutie with the red beard rides backward, leaning over to assure me that everything is going to be fine.

He makes some more jokes about how gingers are the craziest people on the slopes, accounting for an unusually high percentage of ski patrol rescues, considering how few natural redheads there actually are in the world.

"But we heal fast," he says, with a wink. "You'll be back out here tearing up the double black diamond before the end of the season."

"Highly doubtful." I arch a wry brow. "I'm going back to figure skating. At least when I wipe out doing a turn, I don't have that far to fall. And there are no trees the size of my Subaru lurking in the woods, waiting to crush my face."

"Nah, don't give up," Ginger Beard says. "Get back on that horse and show it who's boss."

We chat some more—enough to convince me that Ginger Beard is trying to hit on me, which is cute considering he's maybe nineteen years old, tops—and then we're back at the chalet, where I'm once again ferried across the snow like a wounded warrior returning from the battlefield.

The bearded patrol boys get me settled in the infirmary, where Brendan's torn MCL diagnosis is seconded by the medic on duty, a fresh-faced blonde with a freckled nose she wrinkles in sympathy as she puts my wounded knee through its limited paces.

"Okay, so it doesn't seem to be *that* bad. Definitely not the worst sprain I've seen this week. But I think you should head to the emergency room at Memorial, over in Hood River, and get checked out. Just in case," she says, her brow furrowing. "Do you have someone who can drive you? If not, I can ask the staff at the lodge if they have anyone free to shuttle you over. You shouldn't be driving or putting weight on that knee until you get a brace."

"We'll drive her." Angie bustles in, followed closely by Steve, and hurries over to envelop me in a big hug. "Oh honey, Brendan told us what you did. Thank you so much!"

I smile at Steve over her shoulder. "I didn't do anything except get myself hurt and ruin the fun."

"Ridiculous," Steve says, his expression as serious as I've seen him so far. "You didn't ruin anything, and we're honored to drive you to the hospital. Brendan and Chloe are still about thirty minutes out. The lift let them off at the top of Sweetheart's Mile, and Brendan said Chloe needed a few minutes to rest after all the excitement. But they'll be here soon, and we'll all head to the ER."

"Oh, no." I shake my head. "Seriously, there's no reason to wreck the day. I can ask about a shuttle at the lodge or—"

"Stop it. Right now," Angie says, squeezing my hand. "We're taking you and then treating you to lunch, and that's that."

I text Brendan—who is still at the hot chocolate hut at the top of the mountain with Chloe, waiting for her to finish her "I made it down my first double black diamond without breaking any bones" celebratory cocoa. I ask him to stay and enjoy the day with his daughter and Angie, while Steve takes me to get my knee checked out, assuring him that minimizing the impact of my accident on the group is what will make me feel better the fastest.

After half a dozen texts from Brendan insisting he wants to drive me to the doctor, and an equal number of texts from me arguing that he should stay and take care of Chloe because he's the best skier in the group, not to mention large and scary-looking when he needs to be, the better to defend her from rampaging snowboarder assholes, he agrees.

But not before texting, *Okay, but I'll be counting down the minutes until I get to see you tonight. Chloe and I are both sending good vibes your way, beautiful. Text me as soon as you get the official diagnosis.*

I text back, *Will do*, and slide my phone back into my coat pocket, ignoring the fluttering in my chest.

It's a stupid flutter—Brendan is grateful that I put myself at risk for Chloe, and it's making him text things he usually wouldn't. That's it.

Or maybe he's aware that Angie and Steve are hovering as I text him back, and that "beautiful" was just fertilizer thrown onto the manure pile to shore up our fake relationship.

But even as I convince myself not to take the sweet words too seriously, I swear I can feel the good vibes Brendan and Chloe are sending down the mountain humming in the air around me, wrapping me up in a warm cloud.

As Steve guides his truck down the narrow, snow-covered road toward the main highway, I can't help but turn and look back, wondering which of those dots swishing down the Sweetheart Run might be *my* dots.

Mine.

Neither of them will ever be mine.

My head knows that, but my heart keeps my gaze trained on the mountain until Steve turns the corner and the slopes disappear from view.

Chapter Thirteen

From the texts of Laura Collins and Libby Collins

Libby: Oh my God, are you okay?!
Justin just got off the phone with Brendan. He said you got into a skiing accident after some jerk shoved Chloe onto a double black diamond and you went after her like a crazy, but incredibly sweet and brave and wonderful and selfless, stupid person!
How are you still alive, La?!
Is anything broken?
Can you walk?
Did you have to go to the hospital?
Why didn't you text me?!! Or call!!?
And why didn't Brendan give Justin more information?!
And why didn't Justin ask for more flipping details before he hung up?!

SEXY MOTHERPUCKER

What is wrong with the male of the species, Laura? What's with the just the facts, cards held close to the chest, no need for backstory crap? There are times when a phone call needs to last more than two minutes!
ARGH!!
OH MY GOD PLEASE CALL OR TEXT ME BEFORE I FREAK OUT AND JUMP IN THE CAR AND DRIVE EAST UNTIL I FIND YOU, WHEREVER YOU ARE. BRENDAN IS REFUSING TO ANSWER HIS PHONE EVEN THOUGH I'VE CALLED FOUR TIMES! AND JUSTIN IS TELLING ME NOT TO TEXT IN ALL CAPS BUT I CAN'T HELP IT BECAUSE I AM SO WORRIED MY INTERNAL MONOLOGUE IS JUST ONE BIG SCREAM-FEST RIGHT NOW.
ARGGGGHHHHHHHHH!!!!
I'M SO WORRIED!!!!!!!

Laura: Hey. Relax, sis. No need to freak out. I'm okay. Just a little foggy.
The doc at the ER gave me some pretty intense painkillers. It's just a torn MCL, and I should be fine as long as I ice, rest, and use a brace for the first week or two until I see how fast I'm healing. But the guy who checked me out gave me the good drugs, anyway. I zonked out at four o'clock yesterday and slept all the way through until Chloe brought me breakfast in bed this morning.

Libby: Aw, the sweetheart. I bet she was so scared.
Thank God she's okay. She must be an amazing skier.

Laura: She is. She ended up doing the same run again later that afternoon with Brendan. Brendan's father-in-law took me to the ER so the rest of the crew could stay and enjoy the day. I didn't want my injury to wreck the trip for everyone.

Libby: That's very thoughtful of you. I would have wanted Justin to carry me down the mountain and make a big deal out of babying me and kissing me and telling me he won't leave my side until I've recovered.
But I'm a terrible sick or wounded person.

Laura: Yes, you are.
And Brendan isn't my boyfriend, so…

Libby: Oh yeah?
That's not what I heard…

Laura: What? What do you mean, that's not what you heard?

Libby: Justin said Brendan was asking for romantic mountain lodge recommendations. Ones that aren't solely focused on skiing, since you clearly won't be able to ski anytime in the near future.

Laura: Oh, that…
It's nothing, Libs.
Angie and Steve are insisting on babysitting so Brendan and I can have a "romantic weekend." They know what a hard time he's had finding sitters, so they wanted to give us a chance to be alone before we head back to the city.
We had to say yes so they wouldn't get suspicious about why we don't want to shack up alone together in a fancy hotel.

Libby: I don't know. If that's all it is, why was Brendan so adamant about finding something romantic? His in-laws won't be at the hotel with you, right?

Laura: Right…

Libby: Right. So they won't have any idea where you end up going.
You guys could shack up at a Best Western, or drive back to Portland and stay at your own separate houses, for all they know. If Brendan's looking for real, actual, in the flesh romance, then I think you had better be prepared.

Laura: Hmm…

Libby: What does that mean?

Laura: That means I'm in the car with him right now, on the way to this mysterious, romantic lodge Justin recommended.

Libby: Really! So, ask him!
Ask him what's up with the romance!
Justin and I need answers! And you guys would be so cute together! And we could double date!

Laura: No, we could not.

Libby: Why not? It would be fun!

Laura: It's complicated. Trust me.

Libby: It doesn't have to be.
Come on, don't be a baby, La. Just ask him what's up.
You're good at flirting and stuff. You can get the scoop without it being weird.

Laura: It's already weird, Libs. You have no idea.

Libby: I have no…
OMG! YOU'VE ALREADY SLEPT WITH HIM!

Laura: Keep your voice down! No caps!
If he looks over at my screen, he might actually

be able to read them, psycho!

Libby: okay, okay, but—
omg you've already slept with him!!!!!
When? Why? And why didn't you tell me!?

Laura: Last summer.
For the usual reasons.
And because it was a one-weekend kind of thing.
There was no point in discussing it.
Though, I did sort of mention it that time I
warned you about the dangers of sleeping with
friends…

Libby: Oh my God! Brendan is the guy who said
he wasn't interested in banging you anymore and
made you feel terrible and sad and doubtful about
the adorableness of your vagina!

Laura: Yes, but I'm seriously going to turn off my
phone if you use that word again. I've been
injured, Libby. Have some pity on me and lay off
the V-word.

Libby: Okay, okay. Though Justin agrees that I
should be able to torture you for at least a year or
two in retaliation for the time you asked the bikini
waxing lady to check to see if there was anything
wrong with me down there.

Laura: I did that because I love you!

And because I could tell you had concerns…

Libby: Still a serious violation of privacy, La.
Not to mention the sister code. And probably the law.

Laura: Fine, I won't do anything nice for you ever again! Happy?

Libby: No. I'll be happy when you tell me that you and Brendan are getting back together. *heart emoji*

Laura: We were never together in the first place! And I don't want a fuck buddy.
So, if he's planning to take me to some romantic lodge thinking he can woo his way into my pants for another weekend, after I've made it clear I'm not interested in sex without feelings, he's got another thing coming.
Another thing like a stick beaten repeatedly around his big, stupid head.
I'm starting to think I should have taken those crutches from the hospital, after all…

Libby: Okay, I hear you. But what if he's taking you on a romantic getaway so he can woo his way into your heart!

Laura: Doubtful. Seriously doubtful.
And the more I think about this, the angrier I

SEXY MOTHERPUCKER

get…

Libby: Uh oh. Don't go there, Laura.
The crazy rage spiral is never the answer!

Laura: It's not a crazy rage spiral if there is a reason for the rage, Elizabeth!

Libby: Well at least make sure there's a reason first, okay?
And if you and Brendan decide to date, tell him I'm thrilled and that I really like him, but that he had better treat you right or I'm going to make him a big batch of Ex-Lax brownies.
Okay?
Laura?
Are you making sure there's a reason for the rage spiral?
Just remember that violence is never the answer!
Laura? Laura?

CHAPTER Fourteen

Brendan

Laura tosses her phone back into her purse with enough force to make the bag scoot across the console between us. "Pull over."

"What? Why?" My gaze moves between Laura and the road ahead, but there isn't an exit in sight. "If you need a bathroom, I should probably drive over the median and head back to the last turnoff. I don't think there's another exit with a gas station until—"

"I don't need a bathroom. Now pull over," she repeats, pointing a stern finger to the shoulder. "Now, Brendan. This very fucking second."

"Whoa." A frown claws at my forehead. "What did I do? Who were you texting?"

"You're not the one asking questions, Daniels," she snaps, her volume rising. "Now, are you pulling over, or am I going to have to jump out of a moving vehicle with a strained MCL?"

I reach out, locking a hand around her wrist as my foot eases off the gas. "Don't even joke about something like that. Seriously."

"Don't tell me what to do." She snatches her arm free. "And don't touch me."

"All right." I lift my hand in surrender. "I'm pulling over right now. Relax, okay?"

"You don't want to tell me to relax right now," she says with a burst of clearly not-at-all-amused laughter. "Seriously. I can't believe you've lived with a redhead and a redhead's temper for seven years and haven't learned what a serious mistake that is."

She has a point, I admit as I guide the Cruiser to the side of the road and shift it into park, taking a beat to center myself before shutting off the engine. If there's anything I've learned from my own redhead, it's that being logical, centered, and honest is the only chance in hell of winning an argument when she's riled up.

Any argument, even when I'm completely innocent.

And I'm not innocent right now. I have a pretty good idea who Laura was texting, and I can guess a few things he might have said that would have royally pissed her off.

Which means the best thing to do is confess now and worry later that this isn't the most romantic way to convince Laura I won't fuck up a second chance.

"I texted Justin this morning," I say, turning to face her. "I asked him for some recommendations on where to stay this weekend. I told him we were together, and that I wanted the hotel to be something special."

Laura crosses her arms and glares, but she doesn't look surprised. "Yeah, that's what Libby said."

Not Justin, then. Libby. Not that it matters. It doesn't matter who told her, only that she clearly isn't happy about it.

"I would ask what the hell you're thinking," Laura continues, her cheeks flushing. "But I think I know, and I think it sucks."

I shake my head. "Listen, that's not—"

"I mean, maybe I'm wrong." Her eyes roll skyward as her breath huffs out. "I really hope I'm wrong. Because if this is what I think it is, then I'm done, Brendan. You can take your 'friendship' and go fuck yourself, because I can't do this anymore. I can't—"

"I thought you were in love with Justin," I blurt out, not knowing what else to say to stop this before things are messed up beyond repair.

She pauses, her frown still firmly in place. "What?"

"I thought you had a thing for Justin. And that he had a thing for you." I force myself to keep going as Laura's features twist into an incredulous expression. "I figured it was only a matter of time before you two stopped being friends who flirt and started being something more, and I—"

"Justin and I do not flirt!" A sharp laugh bursts from her lips. "We have never flirted, not a single day in our lives. Honestly, the thought is nauseating. I'd rather flirt with Coach Swindle, and he smells like Circus Peanuts and is old enough to be my father."

"Yeah, I get that now, but..." I shrug. "I didn't at the time. And I didn't want to be your second choice or the fill-in guy or whatever. So I told you my life was complicated and...I left."

She cocks her head, her brow wrinkling again as her gaze searches mine. "Are you serious?"

"Yes, I'm serious. Clearly, it became obvious that I'd misread the situation, but..."

"Around the time Justin started dating my sister, maybe?"

"Around the time he started dating Libby and you clearly weren't upset about it. But by then it had been months since the beach, and we were doing the friends thing, and you didn't seem to like me much, so..." I sigh. "I thought it was too late. I thought I'd fucked up my shot with you, and that was it."

I press my lips together, not wanting to confess the rest of it. But Laura deserves to know what she's getting into if she decides not to kick my damaged ass to the curb. "And I thought it was for the best. For you. I've got baggage, I haven't been in a relationship in years, and I honestly don't know what kind of boyfriend I'll be at this point. I could completely suck at it."

"You could," she agrees, her tone calm and even, giving nothing away.

I nod, feeling more like a fool with every passing second. But I started this, and I'm going to finish it. "And then there's Chloe. I worried about confusing her or her losing you as a friend if things didn't work out."

"Chloe will never lose me," Laura says, with a certainty that sends warmth rushing through my chest. "As long as you're willing to let me see her, I'll always make time to be her friend. She's important to me."

"Obviously." I cast a pointed look down at her knee brace.

Laura's mouth softens. "But I understand where you're coming from. Yesterday, as I was flying down that mountain, I realized how hard it must be for you. How terrifying. To love Chloe so much but know you can't protect her all the time, no matter how hard you try."

"It is terrifying," I admit. "But I let her take chances and push her limits, because that's the kind of kid she is and I don't want her to grow up afraid. But when it comes to my own life lately..."

I bite the inside of my bottom lip, shocked by the wave of emotion tightening my chest. I didn't expect this to be easy, but I had no idea it would feel like this. Like stepping into a crowded room full of well-dressed people while wearing nothing but sweat and my sad, ugly scars.

"I've been a coward," I say, my gaze fixed on the console between us, where crayons, pink hair bows, notes scribbled during practice, Lego princess figures, stick tape, and an empty bottle of Bayer Back and Body tell the story of my life.

And it is a full life, packed with love—for my child, my family, my friends, my team—but it's empty, too. There is a void at my core, and though I have no right to expect Laura to fill it, I'm starting to think maybe she's the only person who can. Every time I've touched a woman since Maryanne died—even something as relatively innocent as a kiss—it felt wrong. Rotten. Blasphemy shouted out in a church, a desecration of something beautiful and right.

But not with Laura.

With Laura, I finally see a glimmer of hope on the horizon, a hint of what the world could look like on the other side of the grief that's made me feel like an outsider peering through the windows of the party for so long.

I take a breath, but before I can find the words to tell her how deeply grateful I would be for a second chance, her hand covers mine.

"You're not a coward. You're one of the bravest people I know. Stupid sometimes," she adds in a gently teasing tone. "And kind of a cranky know-it-all, but nobody's perfect. And I, for one, think your good qualities far outweigh the bad ones."

I look up, the vice grip tightening my ribs loosening a little. "Yeah?"

Her lips curve. "Yeah. Though, I wish you'd told me all of this sooner."

"I didn't think you'd want to hear it. But then Diana texted me and said she was pretty positive you were still interested, so…"

Laura's eyes widen. "Oh, she did, did she? I don't know whether to be pissed that your sister can't keep a secret or—"

"Grateful," I cut in. "I'm going to be grateful. Assuming you can find it in your heart to give a cranky know-it-all another chance."

"Feelings are involved this time?" she asks softly.

"Mine are already involved," I confess, tipping my head closer to hers. "And while I can't promise to be the greatest boyfriend you've ever had, I can promise that I'll do my best not to let you down." I lift my hand, slipping my fingers around the back of her neck, beneath her soft hair, daring to hope when she leans into my touch.

I hope enough to add in a lighter tone, "And I swear never to try on your panties or bras without asking first."

She laughs, her breath feathering over my lips, making me acutely aware of how close she is.

Close and warm and beautiful and maybe, just maybe…

"As long as you ask first. Then we can at least

have a conversation about it." She looks up, smile fading as our eyes meet and the air between us grows charged, electric. "So, you and me? Exclusive?"

"Exclusive." But in my head, I'm already thinking *mine*. She's mine, finally mine, and now there's nothing holding us back. "So, can I kiss you now, Freckles?"

"Yes, please." Her words become a moan as my lips find hers and I show her how thankful I am for this chance. I kiss her with all the need thundering through my veins, and before I can warn my hands to take it slow, my palms are cupping her breasts, teasing her nipples through her sweater.

"Does this mean we're sharing a bed at the hotel?" Laura's hand skims up my thigh, moving closer to my crotch, making my cock swell with the swiftness and enthusiasm of a cock of much younger years.

But she makes me feel younger than I have in a damned long time.

"God, I hope so." I roll her nipples, coaxing a breathy sigh from her lips that makes me want to pull her into the backseat and take her right now, on the side of the road, while the post-Thanksgiving traffic streaks by on the highway. "I want you so much."

"Apparently so." She cups me through my jeans, making me groan. "I have a confession. I love making you hard. Seriously love it."

I nip her bottom lip. "And I love making you come for me. Which is why I need my mouth between your legs as soon as fucking possible."

"Then drive." She rubs me up and down, and my blood pressure spikes hard enough to make me dizzy. "Seriously, Brendan. Drive," she says, fitting the words in between kisses that are growing hotter with every passing second. "I know it's nothing compared to your dry spell, but four months without sex isn't normal for me, and I'm feeling pretty desperate for everything you've got going on beneath these clothes."

The meaning of her words hit, and I pull back. "You haven't been with anyone else since this summer, either?"

She shakes her head, a hint of shyness in her expression that makes me want to pull her into my lap and apologize all over again for being an idiot who read the signs all wrong. "I didn't want to be with anyone else," she says. "I wanted to be with you."

Fuck, she's sexy. And mine. The realization hits me again, the knowledge that there's nothing to stop me from ravishing every inch of her. Nothing except the fact that we need to get off the road and into a room with four walls and a lock to keep the rest of the world out while we make up for lost time.

In a Herculean act of will, I force my hands from her skin and back to the wheel. And then I drive. Fast.

SEXY MOTHERPUCKER

Half an hour later, we pull into the Regent's Point check-in area with the sexual tension every bit as thick as it was before. Meaning we're both strung tight and about ten seconds from ripping off our clothes and fucking against the nearest smooth surface. I toss my keys to the valet but grab our bags myself, not wanting company on the way to our room.

Inside, the lobby is an art deco masterpiece, something out of a simpler, more elegant time, when sitting around the fire after a long day on the slopes was all a family needed by way of entertainment. The fireplace is a massive pillar in the center of the open space, with a hearth on each of its four sides. Hand carved furniture is arranged in comfortable clusters, and bookshelves stocked with hardcover volumes and games in tasteful blue boxes litter the room. Add in the view of the mountain through the two-story floor-to-ceiling windows and the lodge is every bit as warm, romantic, swanky, yet homey as Justin promised it would be.

Not that Laura and I will be seeing much of the lobby, I suspect.

Fuck, I need to get her to a room. I need it the way I need air and food and shelter and a good, long dose of silence after listening to the commercials on Chloe's Saturday morning cartoons for too long.

Mercifully, the check-in line is short, and after only a few minutes, Laura and I have a key to a suite on the third floor. We step into the elevator like reasonable people, but when the doors open on our floor, Laura hurries down the hall, moving swiftly despite her injured knee, and I follow, quickly passing her, even though I'm carrying both our overnight bags.

"Hurry," she whispers, as I pull the key from its sleeve. "Hurry, hurry, hurry."

My hands are shaking a little, but on the second try, I gain entry, pushing the door open and tossing the bags on the floor before grabbing Laura around the waist and hauling her inside.

The next few minutes are a blur of kisses and hands discovering bare skin while clothes go flying. I'm not sure when we find our way to the bed, but eventually I become aware of the squeaking sound filling the air every time Laura or I move.

"The bed squeaks." I slip my fingers beneath the waist of her panties, breath rushing out as I feel how wet she is. She's ready for me, and I don't know how much longer I can wait, no matter how much I want to make sure our second first-time is something to remember.

"I don't care." She finds the condom I tossed onto the mattress and rips it open. "Please, Brendan. Now. I need to feel you right now."

And I need her with a violence that's almost scary, making me fight to maintain control as I sheath myself and position myself between her legs.

"Damn, Laura," I murmur against her lips as I glide inside her tight heat. "You feel so good. So perfect."

"I've missed you so much." Her fingers dig into my ass as she pulls me deeper, deeper, until I'm buried to the hilt and a wave of bliss blurs my vision.

Blurs my consciousness and the rough edges of reality until there is nothing but this sexy as hell woman and the fire that burns so hot when we're together.

I drive into her, harder, faster, urged on by the way she bucks into me, demanding more, all, everything I have to give. And then more, until we're slamming together, wild and frantic, while the squeaking bed becomes so loud and ridiculous it would be funny if it were possible to experience amusement seconds before coming your brains out.

But it isn't, and when she comes, crying out against my mouth, I go a second later. I come with enough force to short-circuit my nervous system, my cock pulsing as her body grips me tight, and I am, for one long, perfect moment, completely at peace.

I don't know what's better, the peace or the bliss, but God…I want more of both. I want as much of it, and this beauty pressing kisses to my neck as she hugs me close, as I can get.

Chapter Fifteen

Brendan

We stay in bed all afternoon, shamelessly making the queen bed squeak until I take a quick break after round three to tighten the frame's loose screws.

"How did you do that?" Laura's eyes widen as I give the mattress an experimental shake, proving it was the frame and not the springs complaining of our vigorous activity.

"Universal tool." I hold up my slim, but exquisitely functional pocketknife with bonus goodies. "Never leave home without it. I like to know tools are close at hand. Just in case."

Her lips quirk. "That's very manly of you."

"A man is not a man unless he knows how to use and care for his tools."

She hums beneath her breath. "You do very

good work with your tools, sir. Excellent work, in fact. I have no complaints."

"Good." I crawl back onto the mattress, stalking the very beautiful, very sexy, very naked prey waiting for me under the covers. "I aim to please. But there's something you should know about me, Freckles."

"What's that?" she asks, eyes glittering.

"I have a hard time walking away from a job until I know it's been done thoroughly. So, I have a serious question…"

Her grin becomes a giggle as I brace my hands on the headboard on either side of her flushed face. "Yes?"

"Have you been done thoroughly, Miss Collins?" I ask, my nose brushing against hers as I speak. "Or do you require more satisfaction?"

"That's a hard question." Her breath catches as I tug at the sheet, drawing it down until the crisp cotton slides over her nipples.

"Not yet, but it's getting there." I claim her mouth for a slow, sultry kiss as I cup her breast, teasing her tight nipple between my fingers.

She reaches down, rubbing my thickening cock through the boxers I threw on to fix the bed, because there is nothing romantic about the rear view of a naked man bending over, and I would like for Laura to keep thinking romantic thoughts about me for the foreseeable future.

"It *is* getting there," she murmurs against my lips. "But sadly, I didn't intend to be punny. It really is a hard question. I'm torn between my need to pounce you one more time and my need to get food before I collapse from starvation, ensuring I can pounce you four or five more times before we pass out."

"Seven or eight times," I insist, kissing my way down her throat and over the curve of her bare shoulder. "Nine if we stay up until midnight." I reach her breast and circle her nipple with my tongue, teasing around the place where pale flesh becomes pink, sensitized skin and deliberately avoiding the tight tip straining toward my mouth. "I'm an old man who loves his ten o'clock bedtime, but I'm feeling inspired to burn the midnight oil."

"You're not old." She shifts beneath me, arching closer to my mouth. "Oh, yes, please, more…"

"There will definitely be more." I circle her nipple again, getting closer to where I know she wants me before I pause, lips hovering over her taut flesh. "But first to feed the beauty before she becomes a beast."

I roll off the bed and reach for my jeans, grinning at the outraged sound Laura makes behind me.

"I'm not going to become a beast!" She tosses a pillow that sails over my head, landing with a soft plop on the carpet. "Now get back here and finish what you started."

"No can do, sweetheart," I say, stepping into

my jeans. "I've seen you hungry. It's not pretty."

She huffs. "Not all of us are gifted with steady, reliable blood sugar levels in the absence of regular food intake."

"And not all of us throw foam fingers at the pizza guy when he delivers pepperoni instead of cheese."

"Pepperoni is too salty, and not what we ordered. Plus he was an hour late, and all ten pizzas were cold. He's lucky it was a foam finger and not my stapler." She pins me with a glare that sends my semi surging into a full-blown erection, making me wish I dared to take a picture of her like this, with the covers pooled around her waist, her hair drifting around her shoulders so that her nipples play peek-a-boo between the auburn strands.

She's a goddess, and I'm still not sure how I got lucky enough to convince her to give me another chance, but I'm determined not to fuck it up.

Especially not with something as ridiculous as forgetting to feed her.

"And that's why I'm going to go kill the wooly mammoth and drag it back to our cave." I hold her gaze as I button my jeans, already eager for the moment when this dressing business will be going in the opposite direction again. "So what's your pleasure, sexy? Pizza from the restaurant under the stairs, something from the bar, or should I hit the buffet and bring you a to-go box filled with a little of everything?"

She scans me up and down as her tongue slips out to sweep seductively over her full bottom lip.

"Laura?" I prod after a moment. "Food preferences?"

"Um, right." She blinks faster, a smile that's both guilty and cute as hell curving her lips as her gaze climbs from my chest to my face. "Sorry, I was thinking about how good you look in just jeans. Why do you ever wear a shirt? It's really a sin to cover all that up, Daniels."

"Well, sometimes I get cold," I say, with a laugh. "And game time would be awkward half-dressed. I doubt the competition would take me seriously."

"No way." She shakes her head, sending her silky hair drifting back and forth across her nipples, making my cock throb behind my zipper. "The competition would take one look at the manliness and head back to the locker room in defeat, feeling sad and wishing they had bigger, bulgier man-boobs."

"'Pectoral muscles' would also work."

"But that wouldn't make you smile." She sits back, bending her uninjured knee, granting me a peek of the auburn curls between her legs. "And I enjoy making you smile."

"I enjoy that you don't shave that patch of red." I bite my bottom lip, fighting to keep from pushing her back onto the mattress and getting my face between her legs all over again. "It's sexy as fuck."

Her lips pucker. "Well, thank you. But I usually get waxed on a regular basis. I just haven't had time the past few weeks. I've been babysitting for this sexy guy I know. But I've got an appointment next Tuesday I'll be able to keep."

"Cancel it." I curse beneath my breath as she slowly parts her legs. "Cancel it first thing tomorrow morning. I like your pussy the way it is. Just like this."

"Are you sure?" Her thighs spread wider, threatening to give me a minor heart attack as she reveals every inch of her beautiful cunt. She is so perfectly pink and wet, her red curls damp and beckoning me closer, that I have no idea how I'm going to resist taking her again. Now. With my jeans shoved down around my knees because I'm so desperate to be inside her I can't spare the time to take them all the way off again.

"I've never been more sure of anything in my life," I say, jaw tight. "Now I need you to be honest with me, Freckles. Are you going to pass out or start throwing things if I put off grabbing food until after I've fucked you again? If so, you need to shut those pretty legs right now."

Holding my gaze, Laura spreads her thighs even wider. "I'm going to be fine, Brendan. Come back to bed."

CHAPTER Sixteen

Brendan

Without another word, I rip open my fly and tug down my jeans and boxers until the fabric is tucked under my balls, revealing every swollen, aching inch of my cock. A second later, I've got a condom from the bedside table rolled into place and I'm back on top of Laura, pushing inside her sweet, hot, perfectly addictive pussy.

She cries out as I shove deep—a sound of bliss and relief that echoes through my chest as I begin to take her, gliding in and out with long, languid strokes that summon more sexy cries from the back of her throat.

Her cries echo the way I feel every time I get balls deep in this woman—blissed out, yes, because nothing has felt this good in longer than I can remember—but also relieved. Profoundly comforted, brought in from the cold I hadn't realized was giving me hypothermia until Laura came along and breathed warmth into my frozen world.

But now, as I take her again, marveling at the perfect way her body grips mine, the pleasure is more than skin deep.

Yes, she is beautiful and sexy as hell, and as she comes, her fingernails digging into my ass, pulling me so deep the root of my cock feels like it's going to be squeezed in half, she makes me so wild I lose all control. But this isn't just about riding her hard and fast or coming so powerfully I see stars.

It's about the way my chest aches as I collapse on top of her, the way my heart thumps harder as she kisses my cheek and says, "So good, Brendan. It's so, so good."

"Incredible." I kiss her temple, eyes sliding closed as I send out a silent prayer that I can pull this off. That I can be the man I've been this afternoon all the time, and that the damaged, scarred, not-sure-I'll-ever-move-on me is a thing of the past.

I don't want to be that person anymore. I want to be the man I am with Laura, right here, right now. A man who remembers how to laugh, tease, and give a woman pleasure without ruining it by turning to look back into the dark.

"Now can I feed you?" I prop up on my forearms but don't pull away just yet. I like softening inside her while her fingertips skim up and down my back, enjoy feeling closer to her with every second that my body is intimately entwined with hers.

She nods drowsily. "Yes, but I'm coming with you. Otherwise, you won't bring back enough food."

"I'll bring back enough. Just tell me what you want."

She shakes her head. "No, you won't. I can eat an insane amount when I'm really hungry. Justin has a hard time keeping up with me, if that gives you any idea." She blinks and the focused quality returns to her gaze. "I still can't believe you thought I was secretly in love with Jus. That's literally the craziest thing I've ever heard."

"It's not *that* crazy." I roll over until she's on top, with her legs on either side of my thighs, granting me access to her phenomenal ass, which I cup in my hands, squeezing the firm muscle. "You two are very close. It's not normal for a man and a woman to be that close and just be friends."

Laura snorts softly and repeats, "Literally the craziest."

"Yeah? What about moles that have tentacles sticking out of the front of their faces?"

She wrinkles her nose. "Crazy, but not the craziest."

"Girl chickens changing into boy chickens."

"Also crazy, but they don't actually turn into

boys, they just start presenting male traits. Which means they might grow a wattle and crow a lot, but they're never going to be able to make a chicken a mama." She grins. "Chloe told me that story, too, but I wasn't buying it, so we looked it up. I demand scientific data to verify the stuff she sees on YouTube."

I squeeze her ass again. "Smart and sexy. Two of the things I really like about you."

"Prepare to add 'can take down an obscene number of spare ribs' to the list."

I nod. "I will. I enjoy a woman with an appetite."

She grins. "Food and sex?"

"Food, sex, work…" My hands glide up her hips to circle her waist. "It's sexy that you love your job. Passion is sexy."

"If I wasn't passionate about it, I would stop doing it." Her hands come to rest over mine. "Life's too short to waste it doing things you don't care about. Care deeply about, preferably."

"Agreed." My gaze drifts to her mouth. "Agreed so much I would like to kiss you again, but then we might never get out of this room."

"Also agreed." Her eyes dance as she rolls her hips in a slow circle. "But maybe getting out of the room is overrated."

I flex my ass, pushing my thickening cock deeper into her heat. "I wish I could feel you bare," I say, loving the way her gaze darkens as she rocks forward, taking me deeper. "I would love to feel how wet you are. Wet and getting wetter when I make you come again."

"We don't have to use a condom." She pauses, her teeth digging into her bottom lip. "I'm clean, and birth control is covered."

"I'm clean, too. You're the only person I've been with in years." I marvel again that it feels so right, so perfect and easy to be making love to her. To be making memories and orgasms and with every passing second, making it easier to believe that this is going to work.

We're going to work. Me and this stunning woman straddling my body with an ease that makes it clear she belongs there.

"Then, let's take it off," she says, softly.

"Lift your hips." I urge her up with my hands at her waist. The moment my cock slides free, I make quick work of the condom and then position myself at her entrance, groaning as she slowly sinks down again, taking me in, inch by glorious inch.

"Oh, yes." She sighs and her head falls back, making her hard nipples tilt up, silently begging for me to come say hello.

"Lean over, baby." The words are rough with desire and the certainty that I'm never going to get enough of her. "I want your tits in my mouth. I want to suck your nipples while you come on my cock."

She obeys, bracing her hands on either side of my face as I cup her gorgeous breasts, guiding both of her nipples to my mouth so I can lick and tease them at the same time.

"God, Brendan." Her fingers fist in my hair, holding on tight as we begin to rock faster, straining closer to each other as her pussy throbs around my cock and the smell of her floods my head like a drug. "I've never felt like this. It's never felt like this."

"So damned sweet…" I drag my teeth over her nipple.

Her gasp as I soothe the sting away with my tongue is enough to make my already aching balls feel like lead weights dragging between my legs. I've already come three times, but I'm desperate to lose myself inside her again, to come with nothing between us, to fill her with the evidence of the way she makes me hunger and need and lose all fucking control.

"More." I grip her hips, drawing her closer on my next thrust. "More, Laura. Don't hold back. Take what you need, beautiful."

She moans as I bite her other nipple before sucking it into my mouth with deep, rhythmic pulls. "It feels like I'm going to break. Like the next time I'm going to break."

"You're not going to break," I promise. "You're going to come. So hard, but so good." A choked sound escapes my lips as she braces her hands on my chest and rocks into me harder, faster, until her breasts are bobbing on her chest and her features twist as hunger creeps closer to fulfillment. "Yes, like that, Laura. God, you feel so good. I love feeling you wet and hot all over me."

"Yes, yes, yes," she chants, her eyes squeezing shut as her rhythm grows fast, frantic, urgent.

"Open your eyes," I say, fighting to hold on until she comes. "Open your eyes. Let me see you. Let me see…"

Her lashes lift, revealing a pained, pleasured, raw, vulnerable Laura I've never seen before. And she is heart-stopping. So beautiful and brave, shameless and sexy that as she cries out, her body locking tight around me, I have no choice but to tumble over with her.

I come with my gaze locked to hers, and in that moment things pass between us that are bigger and truer than anything that's come before. Even in those days on the beach, when we stayed awake until midnight whispering in the dark, we never got this close. I was too busy holding back, knowing there was no way a relationship could work when she had unresolved feelings for Justin.

But there are no feelings for Justin. There never were.

I'm the one she wants. I can see it in her eyes as she leans down to kiss me, her tongue dancing with mine as the last waves of pleasure ebb away, leaving us washed clean and closer than we were before.

And just like that, I know this is going to happen fast, the way it did the first time I met

SEXY MOTHERPUCKER

The One.

"I'm going to fall for you, Freckles," I confess, my lips moving against hers. "I think I'm halfway there, so if that's not what you want, we should—"

"Shh." She brings her finger to my lips, silencing me as she continues to kiss a sweet trail from my jaw down to my neck.

"That's it?" I ask a moment later. "Shh?"

"Shh, and don't be ridiculous. I'm obviously crazy about you. Why else would I agree to be your fake girlfriend, even though you totally stomped on my heart last summer."

"I didn't mean to stomp on your heart." I cup her face in my hands, applying gentle pressure until she lifts her head and meets my gaze. "I'm sorry."

"Don't be sorry." She pauses, that vulnerable look creeping into her eyes. "Just don't do it again."

"I won't," I promise. "I only want to make you feel good things."

"Well, you're off to a cracking good start," she says with a wink. "Now we should go eat before I turn cannibal and gnaw off a chunk of your bicep."

I lift a suggestive brow. "I don't mind a little biting now and then."

"So I've noticed." Her lips curve. "And I'm definitely going to return the nibbling favor, baby. But first food. Lots of food."

"Yes, ma'am." I hop out of bed. The sooner I get my girl fed, the sooner I'll be back between the sheets, discovering where she likes to bite. And maybe hearing her call me 'baby' again, which was nice.

Really nice…

Almost as nice as the way her ass wiggles as she shimmies her underwear up her thighs…

As if sensing my attention, she glances over her shoulder, eyes narrowing. "Don't even think about it, dude. Seriously. Food now. Food good. Food make belly happy."

I laugh. "You're funny when you're hungry."

"I'm stupid when I'm hungry." She slips her sweater on, a smile on her face as her mussed hair pops through the tight neck. "Come on, sexy. I want to eat bad food with you."

I hum appreciatively as she slips into my arms for a hug on her way to fetch her jeans. I press a kiss to the top of her head, silently giving thanks for the chance to be with someone who feels so perfect in my arms.

CHAPTER Seventeen

Laura

Brendan and I dress quickly and swing out the door hand in hand, finding our way to the second-floor bar overlooking the main fireplace, where a man in a bowler hat is playing the piano, and candles flicker on the hand-carved tables. We snag a romantic booth for two with a view of the sun setting behind the mountains and order two racks of ribs, a large basket of truffle fries, and an arugula salad as a small nod to healthiness.

The entire time we feast, the conversation flows as easily as the water we down at a pace that keeps our server bustling back and forth with his metal pitcher.

Who knew sex could be so dehydrating?

Or multi-orgasmic?

Or achingly sweet and completely filthy at the

same time?

Before Brendan, I'd thought I'd had some fairly excellent sex in my day. But now it's clear that all that was adolescent, amateur fumbling in the dark compared to the naked, sexy, fun times to be had with this man. He drives me out of my mind, stripping away my inhibitions, driving me wild, yet somehow he makes me feel so safe at the same time.

"I think it's the dad thing," I say, pointing a truffle fry at his face.

He lifts a brow. "What's the dad thing?"

"Nothing. I should have waited to take my pain pill. My inside thoughts are becoming outside thoughts."

He smiles, his eyes glittering with mischief. "Good. I like it when your inside thoughts become outside thoughts. Remember that time at Babchuk's retirement party when you told him he was drop-dead sexy even though he looked like a scary Russian Muppet?"

"Oh God, don't remind me." I slap my hand to my forehead and squeeze my eyes closed. "One of the many stories that confirm I should never drink. I'd only had three beers, too."

"You shouldn't be embarrassed. Babchuk thought it was funny, and it's not like he's never had a few too many. He was so wasted on a flight home during my rookie season he spent the entire trip drawing faces on a bunch of bananas and rocking them like babies."

"He's out of his mind," I say with a laugh. "But I always liked him."

Brendan nods, smirking over the rim of his beer. "He liked you, too. He wasn't happy when Justin told him you had a raging case of chlamydia and some nasty-ass crabs."

My eyes fly wide. "What? He didn't!"

"Oh, he absolutely did. He also hinted there was something undiagnosed going on, and that the last guy you'd slept with had watched his dick turn green moments after the main event."

"What? What a jerk!" I make a fist on the table. "I mean, I didn't want to sleep with Babchuk—I was just trying to make him feel better about his divorce. But I might have wanted to sleep with someone else who was hearing this nonsense. Present company, for example."

Brendan's answering smolder sends heat flooding from my cheeks down to pool in my belly. "Present company knew better than to believe stories like that. Though, maybe now it's becoming clear why I thought Justin had a thing for you?"

"He's just protective," I say with a shrug. "And distrustful of the male of the species."

"As he should be. The male of the species isn't the most well-behaved group of mammals. Makes it stressful to be raising a daughter."

My smile fades. "Yeah. I was thinking about that the other day when this dick on the train 'accidentally' grabbed my ass for the third time.

My mom has stories about the same thing happening to her when she worked in the city and commuted every day. The way things are going, I can't see that it will be different for Chloe. And that pisses me off. Things should be changing, you know? They should be getting better. I should be able to look to the future and see a day when Chloe will have it better, but I don't." I take a deep breath, shaking my head. "And you know, sometimes I think about being homeless, and how much harder it is for the women who are homeless, and how much more they have to be scared of than men who are homeless. And that's it. Right there! That's all the evidence people should need that equality hasn't happened yet. It hasn't, no matter what people want to believe, Brendan."

"I agree, Laura." The amusement and affection mixing in his voice make me grin, and blush, and wish I'd taken my pain pill *after* I ate six ribs and not before, when my stomach was still painfully empty.

"Sorry," I mumble. "I'm talking too much."

"No, you're not. I like hearing your unfiltered thoughts. Makes me feel special."

"It's the pain pill talking," I confess. "I'm a lightweight with medication, too, I guess."

"So, I'm not special?" He arches a teasing brow.

I roll my eyes as I cup my suddenly empty-again water glass in both hands. "I think I made your special-ness pretty clear this afternoon, Mr. Daniels."

"You did," he says, grinning. "So, what do you want to do after dinner, Miss Collins? We could get in our swimsuits and head out to the Jacuzzi, or sit by the fire and read, or track down a checkers board."

"Hmmmm, let me think." I purse my lips and wrinkle my brow, pretending to ponder the possibilities as I tap my chin with my finger. "So many tempting options. There's also shuffleboard in the common room, I think, where they have the big television and rows of chairs set up."

He hums thoughtfully. "They have coloring pages and crayons in there, too. I remember seeing something about it on the website and thinking I should grab some for Chloe before we leave. Though there's no reason we can't color, too. I'm not too grown up to color."

"Fuck, no," I say, nodding seriously. "Me, either."

He grins as he reaches across the table, wrapping his hands around mine, engulfing my fingers and the glass. "So, coloring it is, then? Just you, me, and a couple of hours of quality time with crayons and paper?"

"That does sound tempting," I say, returning his smile. "It would be funny to see how tiny a crayon looks in your hand. And if the coloring area has a child-size table, that could be good times, too. Large people sitting in small chairs amuse me, Brendan, even when I'm not high on pain meds."

"Large people sitting in small chairs is funny stuff," he agrees.

"Exactly." I incline my head. "So tonight that would probably be a recipe for big-time belly laughs, but I can't help but think..."

"Can't help but think?" His hands slide up to my wrists, circling them lightly with his fingers, sending a vivid sense memory of being beneath him with my hands pinned to the mattress shimmying through my head.

My lips, and more intimate areas, tingle as I lean in to answer in a dramatic whisper, "I can't help but think it would be more fun to go get naked again."

His eyes widen. "Oh, yeah. There is that."

I nod seriously. "Yes, there is. And even though we're really good at sexy times already, there's always room to grow."

"You're right."

"Because I believe in pursuing excellence in all things," I say, biting my lip as his grip on my wrists tightens. "Or at least all the things that matter."

"That's one of the sexiest things about you. Right after your beautiful, bitable breasts, and your fucking adorable pussy."

I dig my teeth deeper into my lip before answering in a conspiring tone, "If I were sober, I wouldn't say this, but I want us to be honest with each other, Brendan. So I'm going to admit that I agree with you—my pussy is pretty dang adorable."

"She really is," he says, clearly fighting a smile.

"I know." I sit up straighter, lifting my nose primly into the air. "I could tell a friend of mine was worried about whether all *her* girl parts were shipshape down there, which led me to fetch a mirror and do some consulting of my own. Because phobias like that tend to be catching, you know. But I was pleasantly surprised. I mean, I know a lot of people don't find pussies much to look at, but they can be kind of cute. Sort of like two hugging newborn baby mole rats, but without the creepy claws. Or teeth. Or eyes. Or a tail."

Brendan laughs loud enough to draw the attention of a couple at a nearby table, who arch brows in our direction. "That's disgusting, Laura. Absolutely fucking disgusting."

Before I can argue that baby mole rats are not disgusting—they're babies, and all babies have a certain inalienable cuteness to them—Brendan leans across the table and presses a kiss to my lips. He kisses me for a long, sweet, sexy moment, ensuring that by the time he sits down, rodents are the last things on my mind.

"Did you get enough to eat?" he asks.

I nod. "Yes. I'm ready to go."

"Me, too." He signals for the check. "But I think we should hit the Jacuzzi instead of the bedroom."

"Why?" I ask, brow knitting. "Are you that easily grossed out?"

"No, I'm not that easily grossed out. I don't want to take advantage of you while you're not completely in your right mind."

"I'm in my right mind. I say weird things when I'm not on pain pills, too. All the time, actually." I narrow my eyes as I point a French fry I don't remember picking up his way. "You just haven't seen that side of me because at first I was trying to be professional so you would play nice for PR events, and then I was trying to play it cool like I didn't have a big ugly crush on you."

He smiles. "I like that you have a big ugly crush on me."

"Then you should take me back to the room and take advantage of my adorable pussy," I say sweetly, "with your big, wonderful, generous, sexy, delicious cock."

He bites his lip, eyes narrowing, his resolve clearly weakening in the face of all the nice compliments I'm giving the man downstairs. All he needs is a little push and we'll both be naked before I can figure out where the French fry in my hand went and why I'm now holding a leaf of arugula, which I'm wagging back and forth like I'm trying to hypnotize Brendan with lettuce.

"It really is the only gentlemanly thing to do." I let my bottom lip push out in a pout. "My pussy will be terribly lonely if she doesn't get to say good night."

"All right." He pauses to hand the waiter his credit card before turning back to me with a stern expression. "But if you start seeing elephants dancing on the ceiling, all deals are off, Collins."

I clap my hands softly, wondering where my lettuce got off to. I seem to be misplacing food at an alarming rate, but I know better than to mention this to Brendan, as he would no doubt take it as a sign of my compromised mental state. "Though I do need to pee before I pounce you because we probably drank a gallon of water, right? Maybe two gallons?"

His lips curve as he shakes his head. "You remind me of Chloe. That girl can't go to the bathroom without announcing it to the entire house first."

"We're just trying to keep you informed and share our lives with you, Brendan. Sharing is caring, you know. You could stand to share a little more."

"Yes, ma'am. As soon as we get back to the room, I'll show you how good I can be at sharing." His voice is so smoky and sexy it's all I can do not to crawl over the table, right into his lap.

"But that would probably hurt my injured knee," I say softly, eyes going wide as I realize I did it again. But thankfully Brendan is distracted by the waiter returning with the check and doesn't seem to have noticed my inside-thought–

outside-voice problems.

He signs the receipt and we slip out of our booth. He offers me his arm in a chivalrous, old-fashioned way that makes my insides go gooey, and we start across the bar. I'm halfway to the doorway that opens onto the stairs leading up to our room when I realize that I've brought my fork along in my free hand and that a visit to the ladies' room isn't something that can wait.

The "gotta-go" feeling hits hard, sending a sharp cramp through my painfully full bladder. I stop dead, pointing a finger to the bathroom sign thankfully only a few feet away. "Ladies. Now. Be right back."

"Okay, I'll wait for you by the stairs," Brendan says.

I wave in acknowledgment as I hurry into the bathroom. Or at least I feel like I'm hurrying. I'm making a major effort to move things along here, but my steps remain sluggish. I shuffle through the bathroom door and aim myself toward the stalls, but it's like I'm fighting my way through molasses. Or salt caramel candy, the kind my grandma used to make that went from sticky to hard as a rock in less than twenty minutes.

But, man, were those a long twenty minutes, sitting there with Gram, waiting for the candy to be ready so we could have the first piece together.

Mmm...candy. I could so go for a caramel right now.

I stick the fork in my hand in my mouth. It

feels kind of strange, to be peeing and sucking on a fork at the same time—but what else am I supposed to do with a fork while using the bathroom, I ask you? Setting it down on any of the available surfaces would be unsanitary.

And I believe in keeping things sanitary.
And clean.
And organized.

I close my eyes, making a mental note to ask Brendan to let me mate his socks for him—when he tossed them into his bag this morning, not a single sock was joined to its twin, which is no way to treat your socks or behave as a civilized creature who walks upright and can operate complex machinery. If you can drive a car, you can mate your socks the way God intended.

"Mate those socks," I mutter as I continue to pee and pee. By the time I start counting how many seconds are ticking by, I've already been peeing for forever, but the rush of water just goes on and on.

And on and on...

Longer and longer until I start to wonder if there's something seriously wrong with me.

I should probably open my eyes and check to see what's happening down there, but my eyelids are so heavy, and I'm still so tired, and the bed is so soft that I just want to...

The bed...
What the...
"Wha happn?" My eyes creak open, only to

immediately narrow to slits as they're attacked by a beam of harsh morning light. It takes my fogged brain a second to realize where I am, and that the rushing water sound is coming from the bathroom on the other side of the suite. But when I do, several things become clear all at once.

One—I have no idea how I ended up in this bed.

Two—I have no memory of last night after stumbling into the ladies' room.

And three—I have no clue what I might have said or done that could have potentially ruined this thing between Brendan and me before it's had a chance to take the ice.

There is a reason that I don't have more than one or two drinks very often. I tend to black out, which means my conscious mind goes night-night while my body continues to walk around saying and doing dumb things without my permission. I had no idea a pain pill on an empty stomach was capable of sending me to Blackoutville—this is the first time I've ever had an injury serious enough to have painkillers prescribed—but that might not matter to Brendan.

Once he's realized how crazy I'm capable of becoming, he'll probably want nothing more to do with me.

"Bad call," I mumble, tugging the sheet up over my face until only my eyes are peeking out over the top. "Bad, bad, bad."

SEXY MOTHERPUCKER

The water shuts off in the bathroom, and a moment later Brendan appears in the doorway, wearing jeans, a blue sweater I've never seen before that does pretty things for his eyes, and a smile. "Hey, there, Sleeping Beauty. You finally awake?"

I nod but keep the covers pulled up, the better to hide my shame. "I don't remember how I got here, Brendan."

His smile softens, almost like he finds it adorable that I have no memory of what the hell I did last night. "That's because you fell asleep on the toilet, Miss Collins."

My eyes go wide. "No, I didn't."

"Yes, you did." He sits on the edge of the bed, making the mattress dip and my feet slide toward him. "You fell asleep on the toilet with a fork in your mouth, and I had to rescue you and carry you back to our room and tuck you into bed."

"Oh God," I moan, my eyelids slowly sliding closed as I fill in the blanks. And realize he must have pulled up my panties and jeans at some point and then taken my shoes and jeans back off again as I'm currently asleep in the sweater I was wearing last night and my underwear.

"But don't worry. I saved the fork, in case you were attached to it."

This time I groan, a long, mournful sound that rumbles through my chest. "I'm so embarrassed."

He chuckles. "Don't be. You were cute. You snuggled against my shoulder while I was carrying you and told me that I was the nicest grizzly bear you'd ever met and that you loved honey, too. And caramel. And that you would share your candy stash with me as soon as we found it. All in all, it was a pretty sweet way to end a date."

My cheeks go hot as my eyes slit open to see him still grinning at me with warmth and not even a little bit of judgment in his eyes. "I didn't know that a pain pill on an empty stomach would affect me that way."

"I figured. But it's really no big deal. I tucked you in, we spooned and slept, and I had a dream about a forest of forks. I call that a good night."

I draw the sheet down beneath my chin. "So, you don't hate me?"

"No, I don't hate you," he says, leaning down to kiss my forehead. "Quite the opposite, in fact. I'll carry you to bed anytime."

He makes a move for my lips, but I stop him with a hand over his mouth as I pull my sheet barrier back into place.

"I haven't brushed my teeth," I squeak.

"I don't care," he says, squeezing my hip through the covers.

"Well, I do. I really, really do." I squirm to the left, wiggling away under the quilt and off the other side of the bed. I wince as I put weight on my knee—looks like Brendan removed my brace, too—but the pain isn't that bad. Certainly not bad enough to even consider taking another pain pill. I'm never taking one of those suckers again.

SEXY MOTHERPUCKER

In fact…

On the way to the bathroom, I grab the pill bottle, twist off the top, and empty the evil white pellets into the toilet.

"So, the pain isn't bad this morning?" Brendan asks, leaning against the bathroom door as I flush the Blackout drops away.

"No, not that bad. Nothing an ibuprofen won't take care of. Or, you know, having slightly less vigorous sex until I've had a chance to ice regularly."

He winces. "I felt guilty about that last night. I should have been more careful with you. Then maybe you wouldn't have needed to take pain meds."

I meet his eyes in the bathroom mirror, a warm feeling spreading behind my ribs. "You shouldn't have felt guilty. It's my knee. I'm the one who knew when it was starting to twinge and ignored it because I was having too much fun."

"Yesterday was fun." He watches me brush my teeth with an intensity that lends the moment an eroticism I've ever experienced while practicing good oral hygiene. "I can't believe we have another whole day and another whole night. I won't know what to do with myself when I get back to Portland and can't find a babysitter to save my life. Let alone one willing to stay overnight."

I spit and dab a bit of toothpaste froth from the corner of my mouth. "I might be able to help you out with that, as long as you don't mind driving twenty minutes to drop Chloe off. My mom and dad are both retired, and they have a soft spot for mouthy redheads."

He grins as I resume brushing. "I look forward to meeting them. I assume I get to meet them, too. Not just Chloe. Since I'm your sexy boyfriend now."

I snort and nod in response, continuing to brush.

"Why are you laughing? I *am* your sexy boyfriend. You told me last night. You said I was the sexiest boyfriend you've ever had and you couldn't wait to ride me like a pony."

I groan again and spit with considerably more vigor. "Okay, that's it," I say, flipping on the water to rinse. "We're going to breakfast, and you're going to tell me every crazy thing I said last night. We'll get it over all at once, like a shot. No dragging it out so you can drop embarrassment bombs on me all day."

"All day?" His brow arches. "Try all year, Collins. You're very mouthy when you're drugged and semi-lucid." His gaze drops as I bend over to wipe my mouth. "And you're very sexy when you're wearing nothing but panties and a sweater."

I spin to face him, leaning back against the sink as I point a warning finger at his chest. "I intend to shower before we go to breakfast, and I intend to have answers about last night before I

SEXY MOTHERPUCKER

get in bed with you again."

His lips turn down hard as he nods. "All right. I'm fine with taking another shower." He reaches for the bottom of his sweater, pulling it up and over his head, revealing his excessively lickable chest.

My lips part to protest, but he stops me by leaning in close, his body pressing against mine as he reaches behind me to turn on the shower. "You said no getting into bed until you have answers. You didn't say anything about the shower."

"Semantics," I whisper, but when he pulls my sweater over my head, I don't put up a fight. I put my arms around his neck and my body happily into his keeping as he lifts me into his arms and carries me into the warm spray.

And sometime between those long steamy minutes as he makes love to me against the shower wall, whispering that he can't remember the last time he was this happy, and the afternoon spent in the hot tub, reading books and sipping hot chocolate and watching the snow fall on the mountains like something out of a fairytale, I stop worrying about what I said last night.

We have another romantic dinner, with one glass of wine for me and two for him, and he takes me back to our room, where we make memories I'm never going to forget.

Even years from now, when I'm old and gray and wishing I'd taken more fish oil pills so I could remember that trip to Italy with my girlfriends after college, I will remember every single second of this magical weekend.

Chapter Eighteen

One month later...
From the texts of Brendan Daniels
and Laura Collins

Brendan: That's it. I'm quitting.
I'm retiring at the end of the season.
I can't stand being away from you this long.

Laura: LOL. You are not quitting. You're killing it.
You're averaging two points a game since you left on this road trip.

Brendan: I don't care. I miss you.

Laura: Yes, you do care. And think of what your performance means for all the other thirty-something men in the league. You're showing them that you don't have to start sucking at hockey just because you're old and cranky.

Brendan: I'm going to spank you for that when I get home.

Laura: Promises, promises…
My parents are out of town from Christmas Day through New Year's Eve, remember? So no overnight babysitting until the party at Justin's place.

Brendan: Another reason to quit and move to a city that isn't experiencing a nanny shortage. I need to do filthy, loud things to you all night long as soon as possible, Freckles. Five nights alone, with nothing to do but fantasize about all the ways I could be fucking you if I weren't freezing my ass off in western Canada, has me on edge.

Laura: I miss you, too. I never realized I could be both lonely and exhausted from not having a second to myself at the same time, lol.

Brendan: Is Chloe giving you hell? I can talk to her.
Or get her grandparents to pick her up Friday after school so you can have a break. I was worried a week on your own might be too much. I'm sorry.

Laura: Don't apologize! We're fine. We're having fun.
She's just seven and full of energy, and I'm twenty-seven and a workaholic who's never taken care of a kid for more than twenty-four hours straight. So we're hitting a few bumps, but nothing we can't handle. And if I get in a serious bind with work, my mom has offered to help out. But I kind of want to see if we can make it on our own, you know?
We're moving in together after the holidays are over. It's probably time for me to get my feet wet as a full-time caregiver.

Brendan: I'm still looking for help. I put another inquiry in with the nanny agency last week. I don't expect you to handle all the childcare when you have a full-time job, too.

Laura: But my full-time job doesn't take me out of town almost every week. And usually Chloe is a total angel. She's just been testing her limits, so I had to be the bad guy for the first time tonight. I sent her to bed with no dessert, so she didn't want me to tuck her in. I got to tuck her stuffed animals in, all twenty-five of them, but not the princess herself.

Brendan: Ugh. What did she do?

Laura: Just yelled at me a little.

She wanted to stay out and play in the snow some more with her friends, but I made her come in and take a bath before we sat down for dinner. We were eating late and I didn't want to rush the bath after.
So basically I was a nightmarish hell-beast with a cold ball of ice for a heart who feasts upon the tender flesh of childhood dreams.
I totally deserved to be yelled at.

Brendan: I know I shouldn't laugh, but...

Laura: It's okay. You can laugh. I was the same way as a kid. I realize I'm getting a much-deserved taste of my own medicine, but...
I don't know. It still bummed me out. I like being the sweet, fun one, while you bring down the hammer.

Brendan: That's fine. I don't mind being the bad guy.
I like it when you're sweet and fun, too.
Sweet and fun and naked, preferably...

Laura: We're going to do this again, aren't we? We're like addicts, Brendan. We seriously can't stop ourselves, can we?

Brenda: Why should we stop? When not stopping is so much more fun...

SEXY MOTHERPUCKER

Laura: But what if someone hacks into your computer while we're Skyping and records us? And then the sex tape goes viral because you're famous and the entire world sees me naked and talking dirty to you and I'm never able to show my face in public again? Things like that happen, you know.

Brendan: No one is going to hack into my computer. I'm the most boring person on the team. Who wants to hack an old, cranky, single dad?

Laura: Um, lots of people, because you're smoking hot, especially when you're wearing jeans and nothing else.
God, I really can't wait to see you in jeans and nothing else, babe.
I'm going to have to exert a serious amount of willpower to keep from dragging you up to my childhood bedroom and having my way with you on my twin bed as soon as you step through the door on Saturday.
What time does your plane land?

Brendan: Noon, so I should be at your parents' place no later than two.
That's good, right?

Laura: Yes. Party is from two to five, and I'll bring the presents for the Secret Santa thing. You drew Jus, so I got him a gift certificate to that yarn store he likes and a case of seasonal lagers. He'll be able to drink and crochet at the same time. You'll be his hero.

Brendan: I'd rather be your hero. I wish I could come home right now, give you a massage, and let you sleep in tomorrow while I take care of getting Chloe to school. I'll text her tomorrow and remind her to be extra nice to you.

Laura: Don't do that. I don't want her to be extra nice.
I want her to be the good kid she usually is most of the time and know that I love her when she's a brat, too.

Brendan: I love you. Have I told you that yet, today?

Laura: I think you did, but I never get tired of hearing it.
I love you, too, and I can't wait to see you on Saturday.

Brendan: Or you could log into Skype and see me now...
I already took off my shirt, but I'm still wearing my jeans...

Laura: Brendan...

SEXY MOTHERPUCKER

Brendan: But I might not be wearing them for long. I'm so hard from imagining you sitting there, texting me in nothing but tiny panties and one of those T-shirts you wear to bed that things are starting to get uncomfortable.

Laura: How uncomfortable?

Brendan: "I'm going to have to get my cock out soon and fuck my hand while I think of you" uncomfortable. Though I would prefer to see your pretty face while I do it. And your fingers slipping between your legs and your pussy getting wet because you love watching me jerk off while you touch yourself.

Laura: Jesus…
Let me lock the door and I'll be right back, you shameless pervert.

Brendan: *smiley face emoji*
I'll be waiting…

Chapter Nineteen

Brendan

I can't believe no one told me this could happen.

Out of all the books I read and the counselor I saw for a year after the accident and the support group for young widowers I try to get to every once in a while, even though finding a sitter for Chloe is a challenge—not one of the voices I've heard talk about love and loss, grief and moving on, ever mentioned there might come a day when I would be grateful for what losing Maryanne did to me.

Don't get me wrong; I wouldn't wish that kind of hell on anyone. Because it was hell. Pure and simple, straight up, without anything to cut the pain.

But the thing about going through hell is that

it makes heaven even more precious once you find your way back to it again.

I loved Maryanne with everything in me, but I was also a twenty-five-year-old dumbass when we met, pre-occupied with my career and my five-year plan and leaving my mark on the world and other shallow shit that doesn't mean much compared to family. I knew she was special, and that I never wanted to be with anyone else, but it wasn't until she was gone that I realized the thousand little ways she filled my life with happiness.

Her hand in mine while we walked down the street to grab brunch on Sunday mornings, her voice singing off-key in the shower, and the little notes she left in my bag for me to find when I checked my gear before a game. The way she smiled when I came home early and she and Chloe were waking up from a nap on the couch—all the little things I took for granted became an unfillable void after she was gone.

Loving her was a song I hadn't realized was playing in the background until it was abruptly silenced, and the quiet left behind crushed me with an intolerable weight.

I am a different man than I was before.

I've known that for years, but it's only in the past month that I've realized I'm not broken or damaged beyond repair. That I may, in fact, be a better person, a better lover, partner, and friend, than I was capable of being before.

This time, I heard the music the moment it started to play, and I'm so fucking grateful for it, even when I'm far away from the woman who's shown me that love can be even better the second time around. Because *I'm* better. Grief broke me down to my most basic, useful, true pieces and rebuilt me as a man who is grateful, humble, and wiser than I was before.

There are times now, when I'm doing some simple everyday thing like sitting down to dinner at a restaurant with Laura and Chloe—just a hole in the wall burger joint on a Tuesday night—and I'm flooded with a rush of emotion. It's so intense it's like I'm flying over the Rocky Mountains for the first time, seeing that untouched wilderness, so glorious and vast that even an atheist like me is convinced for a moment that God must exist.

Some sort of God. In some form...

How else do you explain the beauty of it all?

And in those moments, when Chloe's coloring the kid's menu while she tells a story about a blood-sucking fish she's been reading about, and Laura is smiling at my daughter in between making "I'm about to be sick" faces because Chloe has a gift for the gruesome, I want to fall to my knees and give thanks. Because my girls are every bit as stunning as the Rocky Mountains and the coastline at sunrise and every work of art hanging in every museum in every corner of the world.

And I'm the lucky man who gets to love them.

No matter how hard things have been, most of the time these days I feel like the luckiest bastard in the world. I can't imagine life getting any better, except for maybe one thing…

I'm thinking about that one thing a lot on the flight back to Portland, while Justin gives me shit about being his Secret Santa—"I know it's you, man. I have a Spidey-sense when it comes to these things. So tell me what you got me. Is it a pony? I've really been wanting a pony. Or a hedgehog. For real, on the hedgehog. They're so fucking cute. Did you get me a hedgehog, Brendan? Please say you got me a hedgehog."—and in the train on the way to Laura's parents' place.

"Have you and Libby talked about moving in together?" I ask Justin, who looks as relieved to be home—and back in the same city as his girl—as I feel.

"Yeah, but Libs likes to take things slower than I do." He shrugs before adding, "And I'm sure the fact that I don't have the best track record when it comes to live-in relationships has something to do with it. Sometimes dating someone who knows me as well as Libby does has its downside. I've told her a dozen times that she's different, that *we're* different, but it's only been a couple months so…"

I grunt. Laura and I have only been together a month, and we're already making move-in plans.

It doesn't feel too soon to me, but Justin's remark makes me wonder what Libby—or Mimi and Rick, Libby and Laura's parents—are going to think about our January third co-habitation date.

"But you're in a different situation, man," Justin says. "You've got a track record. And Laura isn't nearly as impulsive as she seems at first, which I'm sure you've figured out by now. If you guys are both ready to take the next step, you should go for it. Though, of course, I have to repeat my warning that if you break her heart, team captain or not, I'll be obliged to break your face."

"I wouldn't expect anything less." I smile. "You're a good friend."

Justin snorts and clears his throat as he hunches lower in his seat. "Damn straight, I am. Wake me up when we get there. I'm going to sleep so the trip goes faster. The last twenty minutes before I get to see Libby are the worst. I have no fucking patience for waiting at this point, you know?"

I do know. And when we finally step off the train to find Libby waiting by her mother's SUV in a red coat and a rainbow-striped scarf long enough to wrap around her neck twice and still trail nearly to the ground, I don't blame Justin for leaving me behind as he sprints across the parking lot to scoop Libby up in his arms.

I would be doing the same thing if Laura were here.

SEXY MOTHERPUCKER

"Laura stayed behind to help Chloe wrap presents," Libby explains as I reach the SUV and lean down for a hug. "They got a late start this morning and were stuck in traffic for an hour, so they needed extra time to get ready for Secret Santa. How was the trip home? Smooth flight?"

Justin and I assure her that the flight was fine—long, but fine—and load our bags into the back. On the way to the Collins' house, Justin and Libby keep up a steady stream of chatter, but I join in only when asked a direct question.

I'm so past ready to see Laura that I'm beyond small talk.

At the house, I jump out of the SUV before Libby shuts off the engine and am halfway to the front door—fuck my bag, I'll get it later—when it opens and Chloe rushes out.

"Daddy, you're back! I missed you!" She runs down the steps, jumping into my arms.

"I missed you, too." I hug her tight, smiling over her shoulder at the sexy redhead coming down the steps. "And I missed you, beautiful."

"Missed you, too." Laura moves closer, I reach for her with my free hand, and a second later I've got everything I'll ever need in my arms.

And it feels so right, so complete and good and true that I decide it's not too soon or too much. I've picked exactly the perfect gift for this woman who's made me the happiest person I've been in years, and I'm going to give it to her tonight.

Chapter Twenty

Laura

I'm a fraud, a fake, an imposter posing as an adult who clearly has zero skills when it comes to parenting small people, and it won't be long before Brendan figures it out and decides I'm not all that and a bag of chips.

I'm not even a bag of chips all by itself.

I'm a half-empty roll of crackers that has started to go stale.

Five nights and six days of being the responsible adult in Chloe's life has left me feeling like I've been ridden hard and hung up wet. And then I fell off the line where I was trying to get dry and was immediately pummeled by a herd of stampeding buffalo.

Chloe is one of my favorite people. But Chloe, infected with pre-holiday-excitement and snow-day-inspired euphoria, is also a ball of constant motion. Gone is the girl who would sit and color for hours, and in her place is a pint-size powerhouse with roughly the energy contained in the sun.

She's a nuclear reaction in little girl form, and I'm suffering from radiation poisoning.

"It gets easier," my mother promised with a smile when I collapsed onto the couch after an hour of helping Chloe wrap packages while she jumped up every few seconds to change the Pandora station or run to the window to see if Brendan was here yet or dash into the kitchen to see if she could steal another cookie, even though I told her four times that there would be no more cookies until after we sat down for a late lunch at three.

I'm sure Mom's right, but in the meantime, I'm in way over my head and terrified that I'm going to let Brendan down.

Even when he arrives and pulls me in for one of those perfect, warm, tingle-inducing Brendan hugs, the worry remains. I'm so happy to see him. The past week has felt like sipping air through a straw, and now finally, there's all the oxygen I could ever need rushing into my lungs as he kisses me hello and whispers, "You look beautiful, Freckles." But I'm also suffering from a raging case of imposter syndrome.

Fake it until you make it, Collins.
You can do this!

You are not going to fuck up the best thing that's ever happened to you because you're not woman enough to swing childcare solo when Brendan is out of town. He's been doing this alone for over three years. You can manage the usual two-night away-game absences and the occasional week-long road trip on your own.

"Come on, Dad! Come see all the presents! And the cookies. There are four different kinds!" Chloe squirms out of Brendan's arm and grabs his hand, towing him toward the door, but not before he manages to slap my ass twice in swift succession, making me yip in surprise.

"I keep my promises, sexy," he says, winking at me over his shoulder. "That's for calling me an old man."

I narrow my eyes, but I'm grinning when I say, "It won't be the last time, old man. In hockey years, you're at least fifty."

Justin laughs as he and Libby pass me on the way up to the house. "Man, am I glad I'm not old yet."

"Neither is Brendan," Libby says with an outraged huff. "Thirty-two is not old. You two are crazy."

I follow them up the path while Justin explains that the majority of forwards quit the game by thirty-two or thirty-three and drop like flies from thirty-four to forty. He's right, but I don't see Brendan quitting anytime soon. He's playing too well, and it's clear he loves the game.

And I love him, so we'll find a way to make it

work, even when he has to be out of town a lot.

It's disgusting how much I love him, really. The way the world suddenly seems brighter because he's close enough to touch. The way my heart starts beating faster and a giddy, goofy, magical feeling swells in my chest when I catch his eye across the room and he smiles that new smile of his. The free, easy, blissed and blessed smile that leaves no doubt that he's every bit as crazy about me as I am about him.

"I'm so happy for you." Libby wraps her arm around my waist as we lean against the island in the kitchen, waiting for Justin to put the finishing touches on our glasses of eggnog. "He's the sweetest man."

"He is," I agree, grinning at Brendan, who is looking through Chloe's drawings from the past week while she talks his ear off about how wonderful things are at her new school (which is really her old school; the transition back has gone so well, thank God) and makes a case for having her first ever sleepover.

He *is* incredibly sweet. But he's also sexy as hell, a fact that moves to the forefront of my awareness as I finish my whiskey-laced eggnog.

"I'm hungry, Daniels," I say, cornering him as he emerges from the bathroom half an hour later.

"Your mom said lunch would be ready in less than an hour, right?" He draws me into his arms, pulling me against him as he slips around the corner into a quieter hallway, farther from the madness ensuing on the other side of the house.

"But I'm not hungry for food," I whisper into his ear, before nipping at his earlobe, grinning as his breath rushes out across my neck in response. "I need cock, Daniels. Your cock, to be specific."

"Yeah? How bad do you need it, Collins?" He palms my ass and squeezes tight, drawing me against the ridge of his erection until I can feel it pulsing against me through his jeans and mine.

I moan softly as I rock my hips forward. "So bad. So, so bad. I can't wait until we get home tonight. I'm suffering from extreme cock deprivation."

A concerned sound rumbles from deep in his throat. "Well, we can't have that. I won't let you suffer on my watch. Not if my cock and I can do something to make you feel better."

"I think you can." I take his hand and draw him toward the stairs. "But we'll have to be quick. Chloe is outside with Libby making a snowman, but I'm sure she'll be in to get you as soon as they're finished. We might only have ten, fifteen minutes, tops."

"Then we'd better hurry." He moves quickly around me, leading the way up the stairs with a remarkably soft step for a large person. "If I give it my A game, I can make you come at least twice in that amount of time."

"You always give your A game, baby." I close the door to my childhood bedroom behind me, giggling as I fall into his arms. His lips meet mine and his tongue sweeps out, saying a sweet, sexy hello to mine, and I melt the way I do every time we touch.

We stumble toward the bed, but at the last minute, I shake my head, mumbling against his lips, "Not there. The closet."

"The closet?" he asks, his hand finding its way up my shirt as I shift our course toward the other side of the room.

"It's a big closet, and it locks from the inside," I explain, breath catching as his thumb brushes across my already tight nipple. "The bedroom door doesn't lock. It never has for some reason."

"Your parents probably wanted to be sure they could get to you in case of a fire." He hooks his fingers over the cup of my bra and jerks it down below my breast, baring my skin to his touch. "That's why I took Chloe's lock off of her door."

"Or they wanted to be sure Justin and I kept our pot smoking over at his house." I arch into his hand as his fingers find my nipple again, this time with no satin in the way. "God, that feels good. I've missed you so much."

"Me, too, baby. It feels like I've gone a fucking year without your pussy, not a week. I need you naked and on top of me. Right now."

"Push the lock," I whisper, already reaching for the bottom of my sweater in the dim light streaming through the cracks in the closet door.

Brendan clicks the button and proceeds to strip swiftly and efficiently, disposing of his boxer briefs and revealing the long, smooth column of his erection as my bra hits the floor. A moment later, he's flat on his back beside a shelf of my shoes from high school, and I'm straddling him, groaning in relief as he guides his cock to where I'm already wet simply from standing next to him in the kitchen drinking eggnog and admiring how sexy he looks in his jeans.

"Fuck, Laura, you feel so good," he murmurs as I drop my hips, taking him deep, my entire body thrilling to the way he pierces me, stretching me, filling me with a perfection that assures me on a biological level that we're a perfect fit. "Yes, ride me, beautiful. Ride your cock. Because he's yours. He belongs to you."

With a moan of surrender, I obey, giving in to the desire pumping through my bloodstream like wildfire, devouring what restraint I have left. I brace my hands on his chest and ride him hard and fast, slamming my hips down again and again, grinding my clit against him at the end of each thrust, while he pinches my nipples and urges me on with a string of sweetly filthy words that take me higher, higher, until I'm gasping for air.

And then suddenly I'm falling.

I cry out his name as I come, my pussy locking tight around his cock as waves of pleasure swell and explode, one after the other in a brilliant row, like fireworks lighting up the night sky.

I'm still coming, my inner walls clenching and releasing like a fist, when Brendan joins me. He pins my hips to his with his fingers tight at my waist and comes with a groan, his cock twitching until I can feel the head of him pulsing against that sweet spot deep inside.

I wiggle closer, on the verge of catching a second wave, when the sound of a slamming door and a familiar chuckle make me freeze.

Eyes flying wide, I glance down at Brendan, who looks like he's seen his grandmother's ghost. Right behind us. While we're both naked.

"Who is it?" he mouths.

"I think it's my parents," I mouth back, a horrified furrow wrinkling my forehead.

A second later, I hear my father say, "I love that eggnog makes you horny, Mimi. I'm going to serve you a glass every Friday from now on."

My mom giggles breathlessly. "We shouldn't be doing this. The kids will notice we're gone and come looking."

"But they won't come looking here," my dad says with a naughty laugh that makes me want to stuff cotton in my ears.

And then some moist, smacking sounds drift through the air, and I revise the wish for cotton to acid. Acid poured right into my ear drums until I'm in so much pain I'm incapable of remembering that I heard my parents preparing to have sex.

"We have to stop them," Brendan hisses softly. "I'm not ready to be this close to your parents."

"And you think I am?" I hiss back, eyes squeezing shut as more smacking sounds and a giggle sound from my childhood bed, where my parents are totally about to get in on while Brendan and I hide out buck-naked in the closet.

I shudder as I crawl off Brendan and grope for a cowboy boot in the semi-darkness. "Cover your ears," I warn, knowing there's no time to waste.

The moment Brendan's hands fly to either side of his head, I slam the boot into the wall with a sharp—*bam bam bam bam bam*—and call out in my loudest voice, "Fire drill! Fire drill! I repeat this is a fire drill and all perverted old people should vacate the premises as quickly as possible. Preferably with all of their clothes on."

Silence falls in the wake of my announcement, and then my mom says, "Laura? Are you in the closet?" in a horrified voice.

"Yes, Mom, I'm in the closet and unfortunately I'm not alone." I quickly slip on my panties, bra, and sweater, just in case my mom or dad decide to come peer in the slats of the closet door.

"Hello, Mr. and Mrs. Collins." Brendan grins as he pulls on his boxer briefs and sweater, as if this is all some hysterical joke. "I hope this won't make things weird."

My mom gasps and whispers something to my father, who only laughs because he also has no shame. This is the man I caught fondling my mom's ass every morning as a child, when I stumbled down the stairs grumpy and hungry and hunting breakfast only to find the two of them canoodling over their morning coffee.

"Not at all, son," my dad says, while my mother makes more distressed hissing sounds. "Just glad you two sounded the alarm before—"

"Blah blah blah blah," I call out, covering my ears. "I'm not listening. Good-bye, Dad, good-bye, Mom. We'll see you downstairs in a few minutes, at which time we will all pretend this never happened."

"Excellent idea," Mom says. "But I will take this opportunity to mention that birth control is an important thing to consider when you're young and—"

"Oh my God, Mom, stop! For the love of Christ." I bury my face in my hands with a moan while Brendan giggles.

The man actually giggles, a gleeful leprechaun sound that makes me laugh even as I wrinkle my nose and slap his chest. "Stop," I whisper. "This is not funny. And you sound like you're twelve."

He giggles again, apparently unable to help himself. And pretty soon, I'm unable to help myself, either. By the time my parents hustle out of the room, slamming the door behind them, I'm laughing so hard I can't stand.

"Stop," I gasp, sliding down the closet wall as my knees give way. "Stop or I'm going to be sick."

"I can't." Brendan swipes his fist across his

watering eyes as he doubles over with a fresh convulsion of laughter. "I wonder if you inherited eggnog-inspired horniness from your mother."

"Gross. Oh God, so gross." I slap at his knees with a laughter-weak arm even as I snicker so hard my nose starts to hurt. "What is wrong with you?"

"Not a thing." He slides down to sit beside me, taking my hand in his. "Not a damned thing. You make me stupid happy, Laura Collins."

"Me, too." I sniff hard as the laughter cramps finally begin to subside. "It's just stupid. We should have been doing this since last summer. Think of all the getting-caught-banging-in-the-closet fun we missed."

He grins, bringing our joined hands to his lips. "That's all right. I think we're doing a good job of making up for lost time."

I watch him kiss the back of my hand with what I'm sure is a sappy as hell expression, but it's dark and I'm crazy in love so who cares?

I'm thinking about how crazy this is—and how wonderful and scary it is that we might have passed in the night and never finished falling in love if not for Diana's text—when Brendan shifts onto his knees in front of me, a weirdly serious expression on his face.

"I was going to wait until tonight, but I'm not sure I'll get a more memorable moment than this, so…" He takes a deep breath and pulls something out of the depths of his front pocket, holding it up between us. "Laura, will you do me the honor of making me stupid happy for a long, long time? Hopefully until we're perverted grandparents, sneaking into Chloe's room to bang on Christmas Eve day?"

My jaw drops and my eyes fill, while shock, joy, and terror burst inside me all at the same time, sending a sonic boom of confusion thundering through my ears, leaving a high whine of white noise behind.

"I love you," Brendan continues, the look in his eyes assuring me that it's true and this is really happening in my childhood closet, a mere *month* after we started dating. "I love you, and I can't imagine anything better to do with my life than spend the rest of it loving you and Chloe and any other babies we might pick up along the way."

Babies. He wants babies.

He wants to marry me, make me Chloe's stepmom for real, and eventually get me knocked up so we can have an even bigger family.

And on one hand, it's a dream come true because I love him, and I love Chloe, and yes, oh yes, I want babies with his blue eyes, the same obnoxiously red hair I had as a child, and elegant, artist's fingers just like Chloe's. But on the other hand, it's only been four weeks, and I spent the past week barely keeping my head above water, and Brendan has no idea how close I came to failing him. To failing him and Chloe and myself because maybe I'm not cut out to be a mom.

Maybe I don't have what it takes to juggle work, kids, romance, and all the rest of it.

And if I don't have the right stuff, then I have no business with this beautiful man or his beautiful little girl, and they should move on, keep looking, keep searching until they find someone better, stronger.

Someone more like Maryanne, who, according to everything I've heard from Brendan and the Gibbons, never got stressed out or overwhelmed or felt like she was having a panic attack when she got home starved and exhausted from a long day at work only to find that the fish she'd bought to cook is filled with worms, the soup in the fridge has gone moldy, and Chloe refuses to eat anything from the freezer because it "tastes funny, like soap and burning mixed together."

"Laura?" Brendan leans down, bringing his eyes level with my no-doubt panicked ones. "Are you okay?"

"Yes," I squeak, even as I shake my head quickly back and forth. "No. No, I'm not. I don't know what to say. Or to think and I—" I gulp in a breath, suddenly dizzy, as if all that oxygen Brendan brought home with him has been sucked away again.

I stand, hands braced on the closet wall as my stomach does a woozy backflip. "I need to think. I'm sorry. I love you so much. I just need some time to think." Fumbling for the door handle, I flee the closet at a jog.

SEXY MOTHERPUCKER

By the time I hit the stairs, I'm flat out running, even though I know it's crazy, and from what I can hear, it doesn't sound like Brendan is following me, let alone chasing me through the house. But it doesn't matter. I don't need anyone flesh and blood chasing me. The doubt demons in my head are doing a perfectly good job all on their own.

I streak through the kitchen, ignoring my mother's sharp—"Laura, what's wrong? Laura, are you okay?"—and head for the front door, snagging my purse on the way. As I dash across the snow-covered grass toward where my car is parked on the street, I'm dimly aware of Libby and Chloe calling out to me from the other side of the yard where they're still hard at work on their snowman, but I don't stop.

I can't talk to them right now.

I can't talk to anyone. I just need to drive. To drive and drive, until I'm far enough away to figure out what to do next.

Chapter Twenty-One

Laura

Libby finds me forty-five minutes later, parked in a corner booth at Wicked Good Donuts, with my Damn Dirty Bastard donut still untouched on the plate in front of me and the coffee in my mug slowly going cold.

She rests a hand on the bright pink vinyl seat with the tiny skulls-and-crossbones painted across the top. "Mind if I join you?"

I shrug. "Sure. Sit down. Have some donut."

"No way, that's your favorite." She sits and reaches out to spin the plate in a semi-circle, pointing to the place where the peanut butter frosting is oozing out of the hole in the pastry. "And look how much filling is in there. And double the dark chocolate mini-chips on top, too. That's going to be a good one."

I press my lips together, wondering if this is the moment that the dam breaks, but my eyes remain dry, and that curiously numb feeling that took hold as I pulled away from my parents' house settles deeper into my chest. "I think I'm going into shock."

Libby's expression dimples sympathetically. "Understandable. Brendan told Justin what happened. You want to talk about it?"

I shake my head. "No. I don't think so. I don't... I still don't know what to think. It just... I had no idea he was even considering..." I sniff, pulse picking up as a whisper of fear penetrates the numb fog. "And now everything's ruined, isn't it? I've ruined it."

"No, not at all." Libs reaches out, covering my hand with hers. "Brendan was upset, but he was also really sweet to Mom and Dad while he and Chloe were getting ready to go. I think he realizes that he jumped the gun."

"They left?" I squeeze my eyes shut. "Right. Of course they left. Poor Chloe, she was so excited about Secret Santa. I guess I ruined that, too."

"No, you didn't. They took their presents home, along with a huge plate of cookies, and Justin is going with her next week to pick out a hedgehog at this breeder he found. She's over the moon excited." Libby rolls her eyes, a half-smile curving her lips. "And apparently we're going to get one, too, because Justin has decided that bonding with a baby hedgehog is all he needs to make his life complete. Of course, I'm going to be the one taking care of the little guy while Jus is out of town, so hopefully we'll be able to bond, too. And I'll be able to keep it safe from Terrible. I'm not sure how the cat will feel about having another four-legged thing around the house."

"Right." I drop my gaze to the oily surface of my coffee, wishing I'd added more cream, but I'm too rooted in my misery to go fetch any from the bar. "That's part of the problem. It wasn't easy last week. There were times when I was so tired, and Chloe was still going strong, and I started to wonder…"

Libby pulls her hand from mine, threading her fingers together on top of the table in a light fist. "Okay, well, I wasn't going to say anything, but since you brought it up, I have to confess that I thought that was a bad idea. And not very cool of Brendan."

I glance up, frowning. "Why? Chloe and I usually get along really well. And I used to watch her all the time, even before we started dating."

"You watched her for an afternoon, or for a few hours while he did a PR event, not for a week straight. You were thrown into the deep end of the single-parent pool, Laura, without a flotation device."

My first instinct is to spring to Brendan's defense, but Libby stops me with a hand held up between us.

"Brendan's been raising Chloe alone for a long time," she continues, "so maybe he didn't think about how hard that would be for you, but I did. I get to send all my six-year-olds back to their parents at two o'clock every day and go home to rest. But there are still some days when I feel like I'm too tired to do anything but nuke leftovers and sit in front of the TV drooling on myself until time for bed. And I have a college degree and years of experience to help me convince my kids to behave. All you had was good intentions."

My chest softens, allowing another fear whisper to hiss in and out between my ribs. "That's all most parents have, though, right? If I had what it takes to be a mom, or a stepmom, or whatever, then I wouldn't have struggled so much. Maybe I'm just not strong enough. Or good enough. Maybe I'm a selfish jerk who should stay single so I don't fuck up Brendan and Chloe's chance at happiness."

Libby's eyes narrow as she flips her long brown hair over her shoulder. "Well if that isn't the stupidest thing I've ever heard, I don't know what is. I thought you were upset because Brendan was a doofus who popped the question way too soon. I mean, a sweet, romantic, clearly wildly in love with you doofus, but still…" She shakes her head. "But no, you're sitting here being ridiculous."

"I am not!" I pick up my fork, stabbing it into the edge of my donut. "I'm trying to be honest with myself."

"No, you're not. You're making excuses to play it safe. The way you always do. But this time, you're pushing away someone really special."

I pop a bite of chocolate and peanut-butter-flavored sugar sin into my mouth and talk around the explosion of bliss. "That's a bunch of horse shit, Libby. And since when did you get so mean?"

"It's not horse shit, and I'm not being mean, I'm being honest." She lifts a hand, uncurling her index finger. "You ended it with Theo when he asked you to move to Seattle."

I stab my donut again. "I didn't want to move to Seattle. My career and my family and my friends are here."

"Fine, but you didn't even try to make it work long distance or ask him to stay. You just broke it off, even though he was wonderful and sweet and you guys were clearly good for each other. And then there's Dodi, Benjamin, and Henry, all of whom were crazy about you, and all of whom you dumped within a few weeks of giving them a key to your place or them giving you a key to theirs."

"Henry was sneaking around and wearing my underwear without permission, Libby." I point my fork accusingly her way. "That was not my fault."

She sighs. "Fine, take Henry off the list. But you see the pattern here, right? The pattern of bailing when things are entering a new stage of commitment? Because maybe you're a little bit scared of commitment?"

I gather icing onto the tip of my fork tines with tiny swipes before dipping the frosting in the mini chocolate chips, and consider Libby's theory.

Finally, I offer a soft, "But Brendan's different. I really love him. I love him so much it would kill me to let him down. Especially when it comes to Chloe. She's his whole world and—"

"Maybe she has been," Libby cuts in. "But that's not true anymore. You should have seen his face when he gave me the note he wrote for you. You're already a big part of his world, La."

"Note?" I set my fork back on my napkin, hunger vanishing again at the thought of a message from Brendan.

Libby slips an envelope from her purse but doesn't hand it over. "I want to say one more thing, and then I'll leave you to read this privately and come back home whenever you're ready. Justin took my car to drive Brendan and Chloe back to the city. He's going to hang out with them for a while and then sleep at his place. I told Mom and Dad we'd both be spending the night here, so we can talk later if you want. Or we can watch *Love Actually* and eat popcorn and not talk at all. Whichever you think will make you feel better."

"How about *Christmas Vacation* instead?"

"Right," Libby says, nose wrinkling.

"Sometimes dumb comedy is the best cure for what ails. I agree."

"So, what's the one thing you wanted to say?" I ask, fingers itching to snatch the letter from Libby's hand.

"Remember when we were little and I was still stuttering a lot? And how protective you were anytime anyone made fun of me?"

I nod, wishing I'd popped a few of those brats in the mouth instead of giving them a verbal lashing. I'm sure none of the jerks who used to torment Libs grew up to be decent human beings. What kind of person, even a kid-type person whose brain isn't fully formed yet, makes fun a sweet little girl with a stutter and a lisp who just wants to play with everyone else?

"I remember one time you yelled at Bart Wiseman until he cried, and then you took me home and played jewelry store with me all afternoon, even though you hated that game."

"It was a stupid game," I say. "But you were sad, so…"

Libby smiles. "And you promised me on the way home that you would always keep me safe. No matter what. Even though you were only nine years old. Even back then, you tried so hard to make the world a better, fairer place."

I shrug, uncomfortable with the compliments, especially now, when I've ruined a family celebration and hurt a person I love.

"And while that's very noble and sweet, it's

also impossible," Libby continues. "The world is never going to be fair, and you can't keep anyone safe. Not me, or Justin, or Brendan, or Chloe, or anyone else. Life is messy and dangerous, and so is love."

She pauses, holding my gaze with an intensity that is very un-Libby-like. "But it's worth the risk. Because if you don't go out on that limb or wade into that deep water and take a chance, you end up becoming one of the numb people. And sure, you won't get messy with the ugly stuff—you won't let anyone down or break anyone's heart or have yours broken instead—but you won't get messy with the good stuff, either. You know? Does that make sense?"

I study Libby for a long moment before I nod, wondering when my little sister got so clever. And brave.

"But that doesn't mean you have to rush into anything you're not ready for," she adds with a smile as she hands over Brendan's letter. "I have a feeling this man will wait as long as you need him to wait. As long as you give him some hope to hang his hat on."

I take the envelope and stand, pulling her into a hug as she slides out of the booth. "Thanks, Libby," I murmur to the top of her head.

"My pleasure." She pulls away with a sparkle in her eyes. "It's nice to be the sister who gives the advice for a change. I could get used to being the not angsty or confused one."

I roll my eyes. "No, way. I enjoy my role as the know-it-all big sister. I'm getting back to it as soon as possible."

Libby waves as she backs toward the door, wishing me good luck.

I reclaim my seat, pulse thready with nerves as I open the letter and smooth the page of notebook paper flat on the table in front of me, hoping Brendan doesn't hate me for running away.

Dear Laura,

I'm sorry. I fucked up. It was way too soon to spring something like that on you. I get that now, and I hope you'll forgive me for putting a damper on the Christmas party fun.

In my defense, I think I've been too happy to think straight. After so many years of going through the motions, feeling half-alive and scared and clenched up tight waiting for something else to go wrong, I'm finally awake again.

Loving you feels so right, Freckles. And beautiful. Even

SEXY MOTHERPUCKER

more beautiful than it was with Maryanne, in some ways, because now I know how precious this is.

And how easily it can all be taken away.

That's the reason I bought that ring—I don't want to waste a second with you. I want to squeeze in all the love and laughs and coming and happiness I can get because I know how fast the good times fly by.

But I should have realized that you're in a different place and that loving me is more complicated than vice versa.

Chloe adds another dimension to this thing between us. You wouldn't just be signing on to deal with my cranky ass, but her occasionally cranky, hard to handle ass, too. And I know you love her, and I personally believe you'll be a phenomenal parent, but becoming a stepmom is a big step.

I should have thought about that, too.

I wish I could rewind this afternoon and give you more time, but obviously, I can't. But I can promise you this—there is no rush at all on my side to move from dating to something more. Take another six months, a year, two years. Take as long as you need to be sure. I'll wait. And I'll be happy as a pig in shit while I do it. I don't need to put a ring on your finger to feel damned lucky to be the man you come home to every night.

But...

Well, I do want more eventually. I want you to be mine. The "until death do us part" kind of mine.

So if you don't want that, if you know deep down that you're never going to be ready for the long haul with Chloe and me, then we should probably say our good-

byes. It will hurt like hell, but better to end it sooner than later. Less confusing for Chloe. And for me, too.

Just know no matter what you choose, I'll always be grateful for what you've done for me. You reminded me how incredible it feels to love someone full-out, no holding back.

It's scary as fuck, but worth it. Worth anything, really.

So thank you.

I love you.

And...I'm not sure what else to say.

Take some time to think, and hopefully we can meet up to talk in a week or so. I've decided to take Chloe up to visit my parents until school starts again, so we'll both be out of your hair. If you need more than a week, that's fine, too. Just let me know. Though, I will miss you. A lot.

Sorry again that we didn't get

the holiday party right this time.
Maybe next year, beautiful.
Love,
Brendan

My first instinct is to rush to my car, jump in, and drive back to the city as fast as the speed limit and Christmas Eve traffic will allow.

Simply reading a note from him is enough to fill my head with his voice and his smell and his touch and a hundred other sense-memories of this man who is already a part of me. Right now, from this distance, my worries seem crazy. He loves me, I love him, we both love Chloe—surely we can figure everything else out as we go along.

But the fact remains that I ran from his proposal.

No matter what Libby thinks, I'm not a runner. At least, not like that. If I'm going to bail on a relationship, I consider all the options and alternatives, weigh my choices carefully, and extricate myself from the situation with as little drama as possible. My breakup with Henry was the first and only time I impulsively ordered someone out of my life in a knee-jerk reaction.

Seeing your boyfriend's hairy balls cradled tenderly in your blue satin panties will do that to a girl…

But a proposal isn't an emotionally or visually scarring event. Even a jump-the-gun proposal.

Yes, Brendan and I have only been dating for a month, but we've been friends for much longer.

Though, now that I know the real Brendan—the relaxed, open, sexy, generous, funny Brendan—that cranky guy I used to work with seems almost like another person. He's changed. And maybe that's part of the hesitance.

What if he changes back again, the way he did after our weekend at the beach?

That's why you should move in together and give it a trial run for six months or so before you start talking lifetime commitment.

He said he would wait, so what are you waiting for?

Go find him and put you both out of your misery.

But instead, I sit staring at the uneaten half of my donut, thinking about deep water and inching out on limbs and how terrifying it was to watch Chloe ski down that run in front of me and know there was nothing I could do to save her if she took a tumble. I couldn't keep her safe. I can't keep anyone safe. Libby's right, and deep down I've known that for a long time.

So instead of adding to the list of people it would kill me to lose, I've slipped away in the nick of time, before "I love you" could become "I don't know what I'll do if I can't keep you. Keep you safe. Keep you whole. Keep you with me when you decide you would rather leave."

I stab my fork into my Damn Dirty Bastard and let it stick there like the marker on a grave, and walk out of the donut shop, carrying all my stupid issues with me.

CHAPTER Twenty-Two

Brendan

The crowd is alive—roaring, swearing, cussing, screaming because they hate the dicks from D.C. as much as we do. And then one of the head dicks slams into our goalie, "accidentally" sending them both tumbling into the net, and the crowd howls in protest.

Immediately Petrov rushes the goal crease, hauling Head Dick off our man, giving him a face wash, an earful, and a few well-deserved jabs to the ribs, while Head Dick shouts abuse into Petrov's red face, something highly original about Petrov being a "whiny pussy." The rest of us surge toward the scrum, which shows signs of getting uglier before it gets better, while the refs wail on their whistles and the skinny one gets a handful of Petrov's jersey, tugging him backward, doing his best to maintain control on the ice.

I'm circling the situation, wanting to make sure Petrov doesn't escalate things by shoving a ref or refusing to let go of Head Dick before he gets another jab in, when there's a flash of red in my peripheral vision. A second later, the butt-end of a stick slams into my stomach, knocking the wind out of me.

My muscles contract and my mouth fills with a sour, foul taste as I spin to see Dirty Rotten D.C. Dick, an asswipe I've hated since we briefly played on the same minor league team years ago, grinning like the dog who barfed in your shoe.

I spit on the ice, fighting the urge to chase after him and show him that I'm not nearly as level-headed as he's assuming I am.

I'm clenching my stick tight, seriously considering answering goonery with goonery, when the refs send Petrov to the penalty box, letting Head Dick off scot-free, and my line heads back over the boards so the penalty-killing unit can work their magic.

I collapse onto the bench—hot, sweaty, and pissed as hell—and reach for my water bottle, tipping it up fast. But instead of a stream of water into my mouth, the top of the bottle hits my face. The flood hits a second later, dumping half a liter of ice water down the neck of my jersey, over the front of my uniform, to pool between my fucking legs.

Laughter erupts from farther down the bench.

My head snaps left to see Nowicki and

Saunders high-fiving each other, clearly pleased with their fucking hilarious prank. On their captain. In the middle of a close as fuck game. At the end of a hard as fuck week during which I've barely resisted, no fewer than three times, the urge to swing by Laura's place and beg her to let me in.

We texted Christmas Eve and agreed to meet up on New Year's Eve day to talk, giving each other space to think things over until then.

But I don't want space.

And I don't want to lose her.

And I don't want to lose this game or be covered in fucking ice-cold water for the entire third period because a twenty-something dickwad doesn't know when to leave the pranking well enough alone.

I start to stand, some not nice or level-headed words rising in my throat, but Justin grabs my arm and pulls me down.

"After the game, man," he says. "If you yell at Nowicki, his focus will be screwed, and our offense will be in even more trouble than it's in already. We'll get him in the locker room. I promise."

For a second I'm tempted to tell Justin that he's not the fucking captain of this team and that I will yell at idiot rookies whenever I feel like it, but I've never yelled at Justin, not even when he was the rookie being a pain in my ass. That's not my style. I keep my cool, choose my battles, and if I need to drop the hammer with a teammate, it happens in private, and sure as hell not during a game.

I'm letting my personal shit onto the ice, and I've been around long enough to know that's always a mistake.

So I grit my teeth, compartmentalize my anger with Nowicki into one corner of my brain and my worry about how things are going to work out with Laura into another, and take the sports drink Justin fetches from the cooler. It's some kind of purple shit that looks like Barney jizzed in the bottle and tastes like old Halloween candy, but it takes the edge off my thirst. And when our line is up for the next shift, Justin, Adams, and I burst onto the ice focused, driven, and mean.

It's a mean game. The other team has been taking liberties, pushing around our smaller players, and the refs seem determined to punish us for defending ourselves. But Justin and I aren't small, and Adams is so fast no one can line him up for a heavy check.

Ten seconds into our shift, we've got control of the puck. Justin completes a sweet pass as I'm headed full-speed through center ice, and I carry it across the line, cutting hard to my right as Adams swoops to the left, gliding into position in front of the net just as I'm clear to knock the puck his way. The pass connects, Adams scores, and the fucking tie is broken.

Now if we can hold onto our lead for another

forty seconds, this game is ours.

The D.C. Dicks call a time out, and we skate up to the boards, getting our end of game strategy from Coach before heading back to center ice. The dicks win the face off, and their goalie slinks off to the bench while an extra attacker jumps over the boards.

D.C. dumps the puck into the corner and gives chase, but Adams anticipates the play and snatches the rubber out from under them. Jus and I streak to center ice, giving Adams two options for the pass. Jus is the chosen one, and Adams pushes the puck up the boards. It slams into the tape on Justin's stick and then we're off, gunning for the unprotected goal, where, after Jus passes the puck my way, I take great pleasure in slamming it home.

A roar of satisfied bloodlust fills the arena because our fans know now it's only a matter of running out the clock.

I've scored the game-securing goal, but I don't give a fuck. I am still a cranky bastard who wants nothing more than to smear spitty, sweaty ice into Nowicki's smug face.

But I force myself to wait until the post-game chaos and showers are complete and Nowicki is headed for the exit before I call his name.

"Tanner, come see me for a second." I pat the cushion beside me as I lean back on the old leather couch where Chloe likes to sit and color when she's allowed to hang out in the locker room with me.

I haven't seen her in six days, either. She's having a blast at my mom and dad's, but the house is so quiet without her. Quiet and empty, making me long for the chaos of six a.m. wake up calls and the hustle of getting lunches made and both of us out the door to get her to school on time. Loneliness is contributing to my foul mood, but that doesn't mean I'm going to take it easy on Nowicki. He needs to get a clue about when it's okay to fuck with someone and when it's not.

"Hey, what's up?" Nowicki sags onto the couch beside me, running a hand over his shower-damp hair.

"Don't pull shit like that with me again," I say calmly. "Especially not during a game. I don't have the time or patience for games aside from the one I'm getting paid to play out there on the ice."

Nowicki frowns as his head bobs up and down. "Okay… So, I'm supposed to take it, but I can't dish it out? Is that what you're saying? Because, I mean, yes, I'm a rookie, but I've played on enough teams to know no one is supposed to be above this shit. Pranks are the great equalizer. Doesn't matter if you're a rookie, a vet, team captain, or the fucking coach. You still pull your feet out from under the table for shoe check, right?"

"I've been a Badger for nearly a decade," I say, fighting not to lose my temper. "I've paid my dues. I get to be done with the adolescent bullshit."

"But you gave Justin the mannequin idea. I know you did. I haven't told anyone but you that I have a phobia about those fucking things."

I nod. "Yeah, I did. It's tradition to do something epic for the rookies, once it becomes clear that they've got what it takes to stick around. It's a rite of passage, not an act of war or anything personal."

"Yeah, well, it felt personal," he mumbles, jaw working as his gaze falls to the floor. "But at least someone thinks I've got what it takes to stick around. I'm not sure Coach is on board, but…"

Fighting back a sigh—why do attitude adjustments always become counseling sessions with this kid—I clap him on the shoulder. "That's the way Swindle does business. Believe me, if he wasn't happy with your performance, you wouldn't be seeing the ice time you're seeing. Everything's fine. Just keep your head down, skate hard, and keep your hands off my water bottle, and you're going to be fine."

He grunts, his lips quirking as he glances my way. "Thanks. And sorry about the soaking. It won't happen again. At least, not because of me."

"Good." I start to stand, but before I can make my escape, Tanner decides to take male-bonding time to the next level.

"And so you know, I think you and Laura can make it work."

I scowl, mood souring again as I bark, "Did Justin say something to you? What did he fucking say?"

Nowicki lifts his hands in surrender. "Nothing. He didn't say anything. I know you and Laura have been dating, and then the past few practices you've been acting like a cactus crawled up your ass. I put two and two together, that's all. And seriously, I'm not trying to be an asshole. I just thought you could use some encouragement."

"Thanks, but I don't want to talk about it."

"My mom was a single parent," he says, clearly determined to get on my bad side and stay there. "She dated a lot of assholes before she met my stepdad. The assholes didn't care about taking things slow because they didn't care about her kids getting their feelings hurt when they decided to bail. But she and Mark dated for almost two years before he popped the question. He knew he wasn't just marrying Mom, he was joining a family already in progress, and he wanted to be sure he wasn't going to fuck it up."

I stretch my head to one side, but the knot in my neck remains. "I thought about that. Thought about it a little too late, but…"

"It's not too late." He claps me on the back in such an obvious imitation of my own bro-comforting style I can't help but be flattered. "She's seriously into you. And you're seriously into her. You'll work it out. Trust me. I have a good track record with this kind of thing. My gut never lies."

Some of the tension seeps from my muscles as a plan begins to take shape. "I appreciate the vote of confidence. And you've given me an idea, actually, a way I might be able to put her mind at ease about the stepparent stuff."

"Good. So, does this mean I'm off the shit list?"

I smile as I stand, slinging my bag strap over my shoulder. "For now. But just a heads-up—don't even think about starting something with Justin. He would absolutely take it as an act of war, and when it comes to pranks, he's out of his goddamned mind. Once he starts, he won't stop until he's got you in tears, begging for mercy."

Nowicki's brows lift as he stands, but there's a glint in his eyes that makes me think he might have to learn his lesson about Justin the hard way. "Yeah, well, it might be too late to take that particular advice, Captain, but thanks, anyway."

Before I can ask him what he's done, a string of curses erupts behind me from the general direction of Justin's locker, and Nowicki grins.

"Biofreeze in his boxer briefs," he whispers, backing toward the door. "Would love to stay and film this, but I've got a date tomorrow, and she likes my face without bruises on it."

Nowicki flees the locker room as Justin makes a dash back to the showers, his cursing interspersed with vows to seek swift and merciless vengeance against whoever fucked with his shit. Knowing Jus is capable of figuring out Tanner is responsible for the prank and plotting his revenge without any help from me, I head for home and my laptop.

Over the next two hours, I write more in a single sitting than I have since college, when I would stay up all night powering out a paper I'd left to the last minute because I was always too tired after practice to stay focused on history or sociology.

But tonight the words flow and flow. I'm possessed with the need to get everything down while the way forward seems clear.

There *is* a way forward for Laura and me. I believe that.

I have to believe it, because nothing feels right without her.

CHAPTER Twenty-Three

From the texts of Chloe Daniels and Laura Collins

Laura: Hey Chloe! I miss you! How's it going? Are you having fun at your grandma and grandpa's house?

Chloe: So much fun!
They have brand new kittens and two rabbits and a bunch of chickens I get to feed every morning. And Grandpa lets me build the fire in the fireplace all by myself!!! But don't tell Dad. He thinks I like fire too much.

Laura: Is there such a thing as liking fire too much?

Chloe: NO! Fire is AWESOME!

Laura: LOL. It is awesome.
But it can also be scary, so be careful.
And don't play with matches.
And don't try to start the fire without your grandpa around.
You know, on second thought, let's forget I agreed that fire was awesome and just remember that it's dangerous and burns can be very, very painful, so you should keep a safe distance and handle it with care.

Chloe: You're starting to sound like Dad again…

Laura: Sorry. I can't help it. I love you, and I don't want you to get hurt.

Chloe: I love you, too, and I'm not going to get hurt.
Don't worry. I've got it all under control.

Laura: *smiley face* Well, good. At least that makes one of us.

Chloe: You want to get on Skype so I can show you the kittens?!
They're so cute!!!! And I got to name them, even though Grandpa says the people who take them home might change their names. But I don't think they will because my names are so good. I named them Chewy, Chubby, Mr. Clawsome, and Chicken. Because how funny is it to have a cat

named chicken?!!!

Laura: Very funny. Those are amazing names! And I do want to see the kittens, but I'm going to have to take a rain check right now. I'm in the middle of planning something kind of urgent, and I need some feedback from you. Do you have time to give me the scoop on a few things about your dad?

Chloe: Of course!

Laura: Do you know if he's afraid of heights?

Chloe: No, he's not.

Laura: What about cockroaches?

Chloe: No. He's a lot bigger than a cockroach.

Laura: Good point. What about flying? Is he afraid of flying?

Chloe: No, he flies all the time, silly!!

Laura: What about germs?

Chloe: I don't think so.

Laura: Thunder?

Chloe: LOL. No!

Laura: Clowns?

Chloe: Hmm…
I don't know.
Clowns are scary…

Laura: They really are.

Chloe: If a clown snuck up on me from behind, I would punch it in the nose.

Laura: Me, too.

Chloe: Really?!

Laura: Absolutely. If it didn't want to get punched in the nose, then it shouldn't be sneaking up behind people.

Chloe: Or be dressed like a clown.

Laura: You make many good points, Chloe. Thank you for all your help, and have a wonderful rest of your trip.
Oh, and Happy New Year!

Chloe: Happy New Year! See you when I get home, Laura. I miss you!

Laura: I miss you too, babes. Sending lots of hugs your way.

Chloe: xxxxoooooo!!!

Chapter Twenty-Four

Laura

Hoping the cockroaches, clowns, germs, and fear of flying are enough false leads to throw Chloe—and Brendan, if she shares our texts with him—off the scent, I book the tickets I need and send Brendan my first message since we agreed to take a week to think things over. *Meet me at this address tomorrow? Two o'clock? And wear warm, comfortable clothes in case we decide to take a walk outside?*

I type in the details and only have to wait a few seconds before he texts back. *Be there with bells on. Looking forward to seeing you. I've missed you this week...*

Taking a deep breath, I text back: *Missed you, too.*

My thumbs hover above the screen as I debate the wisdom of saying anything else. I could say that I can't wait until tomorrow, but that wouldn't be completely true. Yes, I'm dying to see him again—our second week apart has been even more torturous than the first—but I'm also scared out of my fucking mind, and I don't want to lie to him.

So I decide against saying more and slip my phone back into my purse.

I hit the gym, lift weights until I'm dripping sweat and my muscles have turned to hot, aching, gelatinous ooze, and then indulge in a long sauna, hoping the combination of sweat and exhaustion will be enough to knock me out at a reasonable hour. But back at home, I lie in bed for hours, staring at the ceiling, my fevered, fearful brain comes up with approximately three hundred excellent excuses to convince the Crooked Creek Bridge Company to refund my one-hundred-dollar deposit.

But I don't get out of bed or write an email, and come morning, I don't pick up the phone. This plan might be crazy, but it's my plan, and it should vividly demonstrate how far I'm willing to go to change.

Assuming I don't die.

Dying would probably make changing fairly difficult…

"It's perfectly safe," I tell my reflection as I plait my hair into a French braid, the better to keep it out of my face while the wind is whipping past my ears and I'm trying not to faint.

I dress in the same clothes I wore to go skiing with Brendan and Chloe, and then immediately strip and go with purple ski pants and a heavy silver sweater, instead. I can't decide if the first outfit is lucky—Chloe and I both survived, after all—or unlucky—we were scared to death, and I injured my knee so seriously I've had to take it easy on cardio at the gym for over a month—so I decide it's best not to take any chances. I kill an hour returning emails and tidying up my desktop and then another hour de-junking my junk drawer, which has somehow managed to get disgusting again even though I only moved into my new place two months ago, and then it's time to go.

The drive to our rendezvous point—a sports bar on the other side of the highway from the Crooked Creek Bridge Company—seems to take an eternity and yet no time at all. Every second that passes is another second that I'm still alive, but it's also a second closer to the moment when I will step to the edge of insanity and take the plunge.

By the time I reach my turnoff, I'm sweating, my throat is so tight it feels like I've swallowed a dinosaur egg, and I can safely say I've never been so terrified in my entire life.

But I'm excited, too. Because I'm about to see Brendan again. God, I've missed him. So insanely much. It's like the week I tried to give up caffeine, times one hundred and combined with a nasty case of sugar and orgasm deprivation.

I arrive ten minutes before two to find Brendan already waiting outside the sports bar, looking even more irresistible than I remember in black ski pants and a bulky blue pullover that emphasizes his broad shoulders. He's wearing reflective glasses that complete the Winter Sex God vibe, but he slides them off as I step out of the car, revealing hopeful, but cautious, blue eyes.

Those killer blue eyes that take my breath away…

A group of women emerging from the nail salon on the other side of the strip mall get one look at him and stop dead, jaws dropping, before they burst into hushed, giggle-riddled conversation.

He is *that* stunning, the kind of man who inspires giggling in grown women, and all I have to do is overcome a few of my biggest fears, and he could be mine. Forever. Until death does us part.

Which could be fifty or sixty lovely years…

Or about fifteen minutes.

It's not too late to call this off, you know. Just head inside the bar and have a beer. Brendan will never know you had something crazy planned.

But *I'll* know. I'll know I didn't have the guts to stick to my guns, and it will haunt me every day of this fresh start.

No, there's no turning back now. Onward, soldier. Onward to the brink!

Pulling my slinky black stretch pants from my purse, I take a deep breath and step up onto the curb beside Brendan, knowing if I delay long enough to kiss him hello and tell him how much I've missed him, I might still lose my nerve.

I hold up the stretch pants, letting them dangle between two fingers. "This is the best I could do for a blindfold. You trust me?"

His eyes narrow, but after only a beat he smiles and nods, just once. "Of course I do." He takes the stretch pants and ties them behind his head, tucking the waistband up until only his eyes are covered.

I take his hand, warmth surging up my arm, giddy to be touching him even in this simple, innocent way. "We need to get back in the car," I say, giving his broad palm a squeeze. "But only for a few minutes. Our destination is close."

"All right." He lets me lead him back to my Subaru, where I help him squeeze into the passenger's side without banging his head before hurrying around to the driver's seat.

I slide in beside him and fire up the Forrester. "So, I've been thinking, like I said I would." My voice is breathy, and my heart pounds fast again as I guide the car back toward the access road and the terror waiting on the other side of the highway. "But I don't want to talk about us until we've done this thing that we're about to do. I think it will show you where I'm coming from more than words alone ever could."

"As long as you're not going to throw me into a pit of cockroaches," he says calmly. "Or clowns."

I smile. "Chloe told you about our chat?"

"She wanted to make sure she'd given you the right answers."

"Did she?" I take the first left on the other side of the highway and then a quick right, heading for the Crooked Creek Bridge.

"Mostly. I'm not afraid of any of those things, but I keep food in airtight containers and have a standing appointment with a pest control company for a reason. So far, I've kept my life relatively cockroach free, and I would like to keep it that way."

"And clowns?" I squeeze the steering wheel tighter, following the signs to the parking lot and check-in area.

"I'm with Chloe. If one sneaks up behind me, I'm going to punch that creepy red-nosed fucker first and ask questions later."

On a normal afternoon, that would make me laugh. But nothing is funny right now.

Because we're here.

And our reservation is in fifteen minutes.

I may only have *fifteen minutes* left to live, and suddenly I'm so scared my lips have forgotten how to form words, and my tongue is lying on the floor of my mouth like bloated, panic-swollen roadkill.

I cut the engine and sit there, breath coming

fast as I convulsively flex and release my hands, trying to convince my fingers to let go of the steering wheel.

Finally, Brendan asks, "Are we here?"

I hum a soft *mmm-hmmm* and swallow hard, fighting to keep from hyperventilating as I add, "You can take the blindfold off."

Brendan pushes the stretch pants up and off his head, blinking in the bright afternoon light as his eyes adjust. When he sees the sign above the little yellow cottage near the edge of the gorge, he smiles. "Bungee jumping?"

"The highest bungee jump in North America. A two-hundred-and-fifty-foot drop into the Crooked Creek Gorge," I mumble as my mouth starts to go numb and my palms break into terror-sweat, making my hands slippery on the steering wheel. "That's why I asked Chloe if you were afraid of heights."

He turns to me with a confused look. "No, I'm not, but aren't you—"

"Terrified," I supply, nodding briskly as a hysterical laugh rises in my throat. "Absolutely terrified. I can't promise that I won't throw up or pee my pants or scream loud enough to burst your eardrums. Or maybe all three at the same time. And I guess I could potentially have a heart attack. I don't want to be overly dramatic, but my heart is slamming pretty hard right now, and I'm still safe in the car, so…"

He reaches over, pressing two fingers to my

neck, where my pulse is bouncing beneath my skin like a six-year-old pumped up on sugar and let loose in a room full of trampolines. "Jesus, you're not kidding."

I shake my head. "Nope. Not kidding. I'm fine with heights as long as there are guardrails or something, but the thought of standing at the edge of a drop-off and…leaning over…" My eyes slide closed as my throat works convulsively, trying to swallow past the panic swelling ever larger inside of me.

"Swap places with me," Brendan says sternly. "Slide over into the passenger's seat. I'll drive us back to the bar."

My eyes fly open. "No, I have to do this! I can't back out now. I already put down the deposit and—"

"Fuck the deposit. I'll cover it. You're completely white, Freckles. You look like you saw a ghost."

"Or I am a ghost," I try to joke, but I still sound terrified.

"Scoot over. Before you pass out." He reaches for his door.

"No!" I cry, making Brendan spin back to me with arched brows. "Sorry, I didn't mean to yell. I just… I don't want to give up. This is a symbolic journey, Brendan. If I fail at this, who's to say I won't fail at the other stuff? The stuff that actually matters?"

"Laura, that's silly. You don't—"

"It's a symbolic journey," I repeat. "A vision quest, and if I don't go through with it, I won't get my vision quest name. And you won't get yours, either." I trap my top lip with my bottom teeth and beg him with stress-tightened eyes to help me do this.

To help *us* do this.

His breath rushes out as he shakes his head. "I'm not sure I understand, but if it's that important to you…"

"It is," I say, willing my pulse to slow a few beats per second. "I need to prove to myself that I can do this. That I can overcome my fears and change and…jump when it's time to jump."

"All right." His gaze softens in a way that makes me think he understands more than he's letting on. "Then we should probably start by getting out of the car."

"Yes." I nod and keep nodding for way too long while my hands remain stubbornly glued to the sweat-slick steering wheel. "But you're going to have to help me. If you don't mind."

"Not at all. That's what I'm here for." He reaches over, resting his hand on top of my white-knuckled one. "That's one of the good parts of being a couple, you know. You don't have to do all the scary stuff on your own."

I nod again, but I don't speak. My lips are pressed into a thin line, and I'm pretty sure if I set them free they'll do something stupid like beg Brendan to get us out of here as fast as my

SEXY MOTHERPUCKER

Forrester's winter tires will carry us.

With a final hand squeeze, he reaches for the door, and I brace myself for change. Big, hairy, scary change…

Chapter Twenty-Five

Laura

What seems like mere nanoseconds later, Brendan is opening my door and reaching inside to peel my fingers slowly off the wheel, one by one. When he's finished, I thread my hands into a single fist that I press to my chest, the better to keep my heart from punching a hole through my ribs.

"We stand on three." His tone is firm and even, inviting no discussion. "One, two, three."

With his arm around my shoulders, I stagger out of the car, gulping large mouthfuls of cold winter air. It can't be more than thirty degrees, but my heavy sweater is too hot, I'm sweating like I just finished a 5k, and my cheeks feel simultaneously flushed and bloodless.

I find my feet and steady myself, but the world is moving a lot more than it usually does, the horizon line swooping up and down in my peripheral vision as Brendan tucks me firmly under his arm.

"Now we walk," he says. "One foot in front of the other until we reach the sign-in desk."

My chin bobs. "Okay." But it's not okay, and after only a few steps I can't feel my feet. It's like frostbite but from the inside, as my bone marrow crystalizes and my muscles atrophy with fear.

"I had a dream about you last night," Brendan says, distracting me from my rapidly numbing extremities. "You were wearing a white dress and floating in this dark green lagoon, your hair waving in the water around you like seaweed. And you were so beautiful, like one of the paintings Chloe loves, but your eyes were closed and… Well, I knew you weren't just sleeping."

I glance up at him, frowning hard. "That's a sad dream."

He nods. "I've been having a lot of dreams like that lately. I think it's my subconscious testing me, seeing if I've really got what it takes to move on."

I wrap my arm around his waist, offering what support I can, considering I would dissolve into a puddle of terror if he stopped propping me up. "I'm sorry."

"Don't be. It's good." He shrugs. "I mean, it's not good, but it's part of it."

"Part of what?" I ask, ignoring the voice in my head screaming that we're getting way too close to that little yellow cottage.

"Of getting better. Of growing instead of being stuck. I was stuck long enough." He holds my gaze with an intensity that banishes everything but him. "I don't want to be that person anymore. I'm sick of being so afraid of losing the people I love that I can't love them the way they deserve to be loved in the first place."

My eyes sting, and the bridge of my nose grows suspiciously achy. "This might sound silly, but I'm proud of you."

"And I'm proud of you." He hugs me closer. "But you know you don't have to jump off of a bridge to prove anything to me, right?"

"It's an illogical fear." I stand up straighter, forcing my legs to support more of my own weight. "There's only a one in *five hundred thousand* chance of dying in a bungee jumping accident. It's one in six hundred every time you get into a car, and I still drive every day. It's ridiculous to be melting down like this. I need to stop being afraid of things I have no reason to be afraid of."

His gaze shifts to the gravel in front of us, making his expression hard to read. "I agree. But there's a difference between irrational fears and rational concerns."

"Well, yes, but—"

"I messed up," he cuts in, stopping several feet away from the line of people waiting to check-in for the New Year's group jump. "I shouldn't have left you and Chloe alone like that. It was a mistake, one I'm not planning to repeat. I even drew up something we can sign if you want. A contract, sort of." He reaches into his back pocket, tugging out his wallet and slipping free a folded piece of paper that he holds out toward me. "It's only two pages, but it took me a few hours to get it right. I wanted to be sure everything was covered."

I take the paper and unfold it, smiling as I read the heading at the top of the document: *I'll Be the Bad Guy: All the Ways I Promise Not to Suck Ass As Your Single-Parent Boyfriend.* I skim the bullet points, which cover everything from disciplining Chloe to helping with homework to folding small-person laundry and putting away toys.

"Oh, I don't mind folding laundry," I say, eyes mistier than they were a moment ago. "I actually kind of like it. Her clothes are so tiny and cute, and she has the coolest socks. It makes it kind of fun to match them up, you know?"

"I just want you to know I'm not looking for a housekeeper," he says, tipping his head closer to mine. "Or a babysitter. Or someone to help discipline or entertain my kid. That's not why I asked you what I asked you on Christmas Eve."

"I know that." I refold the letter, hands trembling. "And Chloe isn't why I ran away."

He shakes his head, but I don't give him a chance to speak.

"I ran because I already love you so much," I say, swallowing hard. "Both of you. And in the past, the thought of just one person who was *that* important to me was enough to give me a bad case of commitment-phobia. But now there are two of you. Two people who are capable of ripping my heart out if they get tired of me, or change their mind about being a family, or get hurt or killed or sick or just deeply unhappy in a way I can't make better."

He cups my face in his hands. "I'm never going to get tired of you, Freckles. That's not the way my heart works."

Tears fill my eyes. "You can't promise that. I could become a serial killer. Or a kitten strangler. Or a vegetarian."

He smiles. "My uncle is a vegetarian, and I've managed to love him, deeply, my entire life. The kitten strangling could be a deal breaker, but if you're one of those serial killers who only goes after the bad guys, we could make it work."

My breath huffs out. "I would laugh if I wasn't so scared."

"Scared of the bungee jumping or…"

I loop my arms around his neck, moving in until my body presses against his and that sexy, sizzling, warm, familiar, *home* feeling rushes through me, the way it does every time I'm close to this man. "Both. I'm scared shitless of both, Brendan. But assuming the fetal position and hoping change goes away isn't a tenable life plan, and it's no way to act when you love someone." I take a deep breath. "And like you said, I don't want to be stuck anymore. I want to grow and get better, and I want to do it with you and Chloe. I think we should move in together and love each other and see if we can make this work."

The tension melts from his shoulders as he pulls me close and hugs me tight, tucking his face into the curve of my neck as he whispers, "We can make it work, baby. I know we can."

I cling to him, tears slipping down my cheeks as my eyes squeeze shut. "I love you so much."

"I love you, too." His hands smooth down to my hips, squeezing me through my thick pants. "Now let's get out of here. I need to take you home and get you naked. I've missed your body so fucking much."

"Yes," I say, blood pumping faster. "But first we jump."

He pulls back, gazing down at me like he's pretty sure I'm crazy.

And I probably am. But luckily, he seems to love me anyway.

"All right," he says, shaking his head. "But if you pass out between here and the sign-in desk, there's no way they're going to let you up on the bridge. You faint, and it's over. I'm carrying you back to the car, and we're going home."

I nod. "But I'm not going to faint. I'm feeling brave all of a sudden. Let's go earn our vision quest names before I lose my nerve."

Brendan smiles as he tucks me under his arm again. "What's your name going to be? Pees

When She Screams?"

"If you're lucky. It might be Pukes While She Screams. Considering you're going to be jumping right next to me, Daniels, that could get really gross for you really fast."

He shudders and hugs me closer. "I must really love you."

I lean my head on his shoulder. "You really must. Because I'm not kidding. This could get messy."

"I know," he says softly. "But I'm not afraid of making messes. Or helping to clean them up. As long as you're there with me."

It's such a romantic, wonderful thing to say I can't resist the urge to turn to him, stealing a kiss that becomes two kisses, and then three, because once we start, neither of us wants to stop. We make out covertly—short, sweet kisses and longer, deeper ones that probably qualify as PDA violations—as we shuffle from the back of the line to the front.

At the counter, I manage to give my name and confirmation info to the bright-eyed, man-bunned dude in an only slightly breathy voice. Fifteen minutes later, we're strapped into thick harnesses that seem to be taking safety seriously and climbing onto the backs of two heavily modified pickup trucks with matching platforms that extend over the edge of the bridge.

There are twelve jumpers total, and we'll be flying over the edge in groups of two. But thanks to the twenty Brendan slipped our jump operators on the way across the bridge—having correctly deduced that the chances of me passing out would increase with every couple we had to watch plummet before it was our turn—we're going first.

"Keep your eyes on me until the last second," Brendan says, voice raised to be heard over the wind whipping through the gorge.

My head bobs up and down as I inch toward the edge, knees slightly bent and arms held out to my sides like I'm balancing on a wire instead of plodding slowly down a platform at least seven feet across.

My handler chuckles beside me and says in a friendly baritone, "You're going to be fine. It's wicked fun. You'll be back here next weekend, begging to go again."

I hum doubtfully but can't speak. My throat is too tight, and my ribs have decided not to expand for more than a shallow wheeze. My heart is slam-dancing in my chest, and the squeaky fear-voice in my brain is screeching "Run away! Run away!" The only thing keeping me from dropping to my knees and begging someone to help me back to the car is Brendan's steady blue gaze.

He doesn't say another word, but in his eyes I see everything I need.

His eyes say—
You can do this.
But if you can't it's okay.

Whatever you choose, I'm here with you.
Because I believe in you.
And I love you.
And you're not alone.

And for the first time in my life, change isn't as scary as the thought of not being with this person. This strong, sweet, brave, incredible person who I love with my entire heart, and who loves me just the way I am.

"Love you," I mouth as we reach the edge and our feet are wrapped up for the final plunge.

"Love you, too," Brendan mouths back with a grin and a nod toward the great unknown.

My heart does a swan dive in my chest, making it feel like part of me is already falling as I nod back.

Falling…

Falling…

And then, with our eyes still locked, Brendan and I bend our knees, brace ourselves, and…

Fly.

EPILOGUE

The following summer...
Brendan

"Hurry!" Chloe pinwheels her arm, eyes wide and impatient. "We're going to miss the sunset if we don't hurry!"

"You run ahead and find us a spot," I say. "Just stay back from the edge until Laura and I get there."

"And make sure you pull your kite in and hold on tight before you climb up," Laura adds. "The wind is stronger up there."

"Got it!" Chloe gives Laura a thumbs-up before dashing down the beach, pulling her mermaid kite behind her, her braids bouncing as her bare feet smack the damp sand.

Beside me, my other favorite redhead is looking ridiculously sexy in a green swimsuit cover-up that barely conceals her ass, granting me peekaboo glimpses of the black bikini underneath as the wind whips along the coast. I'm already counting the hours until it's time to tuck Chloe in with the rest of the kids spending the night at the beach home Justin rented for his birthday. Then we can retreat to our private room where I will demonstrate my continued commitment to making Laura come again and again until she's so exhausted I'll have to carry her to the shower to clean up before bed.

"Stop it," she whispers, a grin stretching across her face.

"Stop what?" I reach over to cup her ass as we walk, unable to resist the lure of her fine as hell backside.

She puts her hand to my chest, playfully pushing me away. "That. You're going to gross Chloe out again."

"Chloe is going to have to get over it." I wrap my arm around Laura's waist, pulling her close. "I can't be expected to keep my hands to myself when you walk around looking like that."

She laughs. "So it's my fault that you have zero self-control?"

"Completely your fault." I pat her ass affectionately, pleased when she doesn't pull away. "But I do have some self-control. I'm not dragging you into that cave over there and having my way with you, for example."

"Well, that's good." She leans into me. "Then we would miss the sunset for sure, and Chloe would be really mad."

"What would we do without her to keep us in line?" I smile as Chloe turns, as if on cue, and pinwheels her arm again, clearly displeased with the speed of our progress down the beach.

"Fall to ruin," Laura says seriously. "Fall to ruin and miss sunsets and not be the first people in line for brunch at the Farm on Sundays."

I grunt softly. "Remind me to set her clock back an hour after she's asleep next Saturday. I would really like to sleep in once or twice before practice starts up again."

"Next Saturday she'll be at Steve and Angie's for her summer visit," Laura says, a sly note in her voice. "And I was thinking maybe we could slip away for a trip, too."

"Sounds good. A trip where?"

"You'll see," she says mysteriously as she sets off at a trot after Chloe. "Come on! The view's supposed to be gorgeous from the lookout point."

I hesitate a moment, watching the two people I love most running away down the sand, their red hair lit up with gold in the fading light, my heart twisting in my chest. Even now, six months into living and loving together full-time, there are still moments when this kind of happiness is a shock to my system.

When I can't believe that both of those beautiful girls are mine.

That they're my family, and they love me, and

more importantly, they let me love them. No holding back. No hiding. No keeping it toned down or tamed, or pretending I'm not a sappy bastard who gets tears in his eyes at weird moments when it hits me all over again how lucky I am.

I know someday things will get hard again. Someday that little girl I love will grow and change the way she's changed before, becoming someone different than the sweet, snuffly baby who slept on my chest, or the toddler who squealed with delight when I launched her into the air above my head so she could fly. This version of Chloe will pass away, gone forever. It hurts to know how short my time with each incarnation of her will be, but it's also part of what makes every second so precious.

Someday Laura and I will change, too—slower than the lightning flash of a baby growing into a wild, silly, wonderful girl, but we'll still be different.

But we'll be different together, our relationship growing deeper, closer, finer with time. I know this way I know the sea is salty and the sun will slip below the horizon when the day is through. It's a truth settled deep in my bones, easing the need to hurry to the next step.

We'll get there.

There's no need to rush. No need at all.

The thought is fresh in my mind as I jog up the rocky trail to the cliff, reaching the top as the sun is kissing the waves but finding the lookout area oddly deserted. There's no one here, in fact, except Chloe, Laura, and a table set for three, a white tablecloth secured to its legs with brown twine, plates covered with silver domes, and a vase of flowers fluttering in the breeze.

"Surprise!" Chloe shouts, jumping up and down, waving her kite overhead. "We tricked you!"

"We didn't trick him," Laura says, laughing as she tugs Chloe's braid. "It's only a trick if there's something bad at the end of the surprise."

Chloe grins. "But it's still fun. You should see your face, Dad. You're totally surprised. You had no idea we had a secret!"

"I didn't," I confess, moving to help Laura secure Chloe's kite beneath the legs of one of the chairs. "So, what's the celebration for, ladies?"

"Just for fun," Chloe says, patting my arm. "Because we like you."

My heart twists again. "Well, thank you. I like you an awful lot, too."

"Actually, that's not completely true." Laura moves to stand on the opposite side of the table, resting her hands on the back of one of the chairs. "I have a confession to make, Chloe. Part of this surprise is for you."

"You double-crossed me?" Chloe climbs into the chair beside me, sitting on her knees, clearly excited.

"Sorry, but it's for a good reason." Laura

smiles as her fingers play nervously back and forth across the wood. "I have an important question I need to ask you and your dad, and I wanted it to be something special we would always remember."

This time, my heart doesn't twist. It leaps and dives, then stops for a long, breathless beat, making time slow to a crawl as Laura plucks a slim white jewelry box that I didn't notice before from the table.

A voice in my head warns that this might not be what I think it is, but I ignore it. That voice is the old voice, the fearful voice, the one that's too clenched and cautious to realize this is the real thing, the kind of love that comes around once in a lifetime. Maybe twice if you're very brave and very lucky and meet someone as wonderful as the woman standing in front of me holding a ring in one hand and a delicate silver necklace in the other.

Laura looks up, our eyes meet over the table, and we smile—and it's suddenly all I can do not to swoop her up in my arms and kiss her until there's no doubt about my answer.

But instead, I force myself to wait for the question, the one I can't wait to hear.

Laura

His smile…

His ridiculously beautiful smile…

It tells me everything I need to know, but there's still so much to say, so many things I want these two people who have become my world to know. They are my family, my home, my safe place, no matter how rough a day I've had at work, or how many scary things are going on in the world.

Now, if I can manage to keep from bursting into tears before I get all my words out.

"Brendan and Chloe," I begin, willing my throat to relax. "I love you both so much. Sometimes I still can't believe that I get to live with two such kind, silly, wonderfully weird people who make me laugh and think and are always there when I need a hug."

"Or a kiss." Chloe nudges Brendan with an elbow, but her dancing eyes stay trained on me, clearly intrigued by my "double cross" and what my speech might be leading up to.

I nod. "Yes, or a kiss. What I'm trying to say is that I feel lucky. So very lucky. And that I'm hoping we can make this official." I shift from one foot to the other, nervous, though I'm sure at least one of the people I love is going to say yes.

With a deep breath, I hold up the simple platinum ring I bought last month and have been saving for the right moment. "Brendan, you make me happier than I thought I could be. Every day, in a hundred different ways, you remind me that I am loved, special, and appreciated. I wake up excited to see the sun rise in a way I've never been before because it means I get to share another day with you and our girl."

His eyes start to shine, which makes my nose burn, and before I know it, tears are slipping down my cheeks. But I'm smiling, too, because Brendan is already nodding yes, even before I add, "The only way life could get any better is if maybe you would agree to be my husband? Maybe?"

"Yes, yes, and hell yes." He snatches me up in a hug, squeezing me so tight I start to laugh with relief and a bone-deep gratitude that helps banish the last of my nerves as Brendan sets me back on my feet.

"My next question is for you, Chloe." I turn to her, holding up the necklace with the two hearts entwined—one little and one big—that I hope will always make her think of us and how much I love her. "Would you do me the very great honor of being my stepdaughter?"

"Forever?" she asks, eyes wide as she blinks up at me.

"Yes," I promise. "Or as close to it as we can get. I know you'll be in my heart forever. Do you think that will be good enough?"

She nods slowly, her chin dimpling as she reaches for the necklace only to pull her hands away at the last second. "Will you put it on for me?" There's a shy note in her voice I'm not used to, that makes it even harder to keep from snotting all over myself.

"Yes, I will. It would be my pleasure." I brush her braids out of the way and guide the necklace around her neck. I'm still bleary-eyed, so it takes a couple of tries, but finally I get the clasp to catch, and Chloe smiles, beaming up at Brendan.

"Look Dad." She brings her hand to the necklace, touching it gently.

"I see." Brendan sniffs as he swipes a thumb under his eye. "It's beautiful, baby."

"You're crying," Chloe says accusingly, brows furrowing.

"I'm just really happy," he says, laugh-sniffing as he loops his arms around me from behind. "Very, very happy." He kisses the top of my head. "Now we only need one more thing, and we'll be ready to go."

"What's that?" Chloe asks as she spins the charm between her fingers. "Dinner and extra dessert?"

Brendan and I both laugh-sniff at that one.

"Yes, dinner and dessert," he agrees. "And a ring for Laura. Luckily, I happen to have one of those back at the house."

"Or it might be in your luggage." I turn in his arms. "Where I put it in case you didn't want to be the only one sporting an engagement ring at breakfast tomorrow."

Brendan smiles, clearly pleased and happy and in love with me, which is still a miraculous turn of events I'm thankful for every day. "Sexy and smart. And beautiful. And thoughtful. And good to me and my baby. How did I get so lucky, Freckles?"

"I'm not a baby!" Chloe announces firmly, making Brendan and I smile again.

"Absolutely not." I wink at Brendan before adding in a softer voice, "Diana will be here in about forty-five minutes to get Chloe, so we should probably eat. I thought we might want to stay and watch the stars come out over a bottle of champagne I happen to have stored in a cooler beneath the table."

"You are so sexy right now," he says with a soft growl.

"Ew, stop," Chloe says, but she's grinning as she climbs back into her seat at the table. "I'm getting ready to eat, for goodness sake."

"I can't help it." Brendan pats my ass one last time before he pulls out my chair. "I'm crazy in love with your future stepmom."

"Do I get to be the flower girl?" Chloe's eyes light up like she just spotted a mermaid unicorn swimming in the waves behind us. "At the wedding? I do, right? Who else would you pick?"

The next thirty minutes we spend watching the sun set and eating grilled shrimp salad with mango dressing—Chloe's favorite—while discussing the flower girl dress, which is clearly a much more pressing concern than what the bride will be wearing to the wedding, and whether or not crowns of flowers will be mandatory attire for anyone wishing to attend this celebration. We end the meal with giant blueberry muffins with sugar baked into the top, another of Chloe's favorites, and a treat that qualifies as "double dessert," and are finishing up just as Diana appears on the path leading up to the lookout point.

"Looks like congratulations are in order," she says, holding one arm out to Brendan while the other reaches my way. "Bring it in here, you two. I'm so happy for you! It couldn't happen to two more wonderful people."

"And me, too," Chloe adds. "I got a necklace!"

Diana makes some appropriately impressed sounds over Chloe's new necklace, and then, after some very sweet kisses and hugs from our favorite nearly-eight-year-old, Brendan and I are finally alone.

"Thank you." His fingers glide into my hair as I step into his arms. "For including her. It made it so special. She's never going to forget that she was a part of this, of the day we promised to be a family."

I sniff, pressing my lips together as my eyes start to fill again. "You're welcome, but you have to stop or I'm going to cry again."

"That's okay. You're sexy when you cry," he says, making me laugh. I'm still smiling when his lips meet mine, but soon laughter is the last thing on my mind as Brendan's tongue strokes into my mouth and his fingers tease along the place where my bikini bottom meets my skin.

"We can't," I mumble against his lips. "Someone might see."

"No, they won't." His fingers slip beneath my

suit, teasing closer to where I ache for him. "It's almost dark."

"But it's not dark yet." I lean back, placing a hand on his chest. "And I haven't had a single glass of champagne."

"But if I give you champagne, you'll agree to anything, Freckles."

"Exactly," I whisper, smiling up at him as I wiggle my eyebrows suggestively.

His eyes glitter, and his lips curve into a wicked grin. "As long as you won't accuse me of taking advantage when you're sober tomorrow morning."

"The only thing I'll accuse you of is being a coward if you refuse to get me tipsy and do naughty things to me under the stars."

"Consider it done, baby," he promises.

After two glasses of champagne shared on a large flat rock with a killer view of the waves going dark as the stars wink on in the sky and fires flicker to life on the beach, Brendan pulls me onto his lap, guiding my knees to either side of his hips. And then his hands are everywhere.

He unbuttons my cover-up and pulls my bikini top down, baring my breasts, teasing my nipples as his lips devour mine. The waves crash, and my head spins because I am drunk on love and desire and this beautiful man who will one day soon be my husband.

"Let's elope," I say as he pulls the ties at either side of my bottoms and quickly draws the fabric from between my legs. "Next week. You, me, and Las Vegas. Or Mexico. Wherever we can get it done the fastest."

"No, we're going to do it right." His breath rushes out over my lips as he frees his cocks and guides me down onto his hot length. "I'm going to marry you in front of our friends and family and a photographer I know who takes incredible pictures of my beautiful wife."

"I can't wait." I sigh into him as he fills me perfectly, completely, and my body welcomes him in like the dear friend he is. "I can't wait to be your wife."

"How about Christmas?" he asks as we begin to move. "On top of a mountain, with snow in your hair like a Viking princess? And then I'll take you to the honeymoon suite and start working on getting you knocked up."

"Yes." I moan, the thought of babies no longer scary.

It's simply beautiful. Exciting. And weirdly...sexy.

So sexy that it isn't long before I'm at the edge, clinging to Brendan's shoulders as I ride him harder, faster, the magic surging between us the way it always does.

My head falls back, the stars spinning as I come in thick, dizzy waves. Brendan joins me a second later, calling out my name as he pulls me close, closer, closest, until our hearts are beating in time and our blood hums in tune beneath our sweat-slick skin.

And even though I nearly fall and twist my ankle later, stumbling down the trail to the beach in the dark while tipsy on champagne and love, it is the best night ever. The very best.

Sure to be followed by many even better nights to come.

The End

Keep reading for a free excerpt of Puck Aholic, Tanner and Diana's story!

Acknowledgements

First and foremost, thank you to my readers. Every email and post on my Facebook page have meant so much. I can't express how deeply grateful I am for the chance to entertain you.

More big thanks to my Street Team, who I am convinced are the sweetest, funniest, kindest group of people around. You inspire me and keep me going and I'm not sure I'd be one-third as productive without you. Big tackle hugs to all.

More thanks to the Facebook groups who have welcomed me in, to the bloggers who have taken a chance on a newbie, and to everyone who has taken time out of their day to write and post a review.

And of course, many thanks to my husband, who not only loves me well but also supports me in everything I do. I don't know how I got so lucky, man, but I am hanging on tight to you.

Tell Lili your favorite part!

I love reading your thoughts about the books and your review matters. Reviews help readers find new-to-them authors to enjoy. So if you could take a moment to leave a review letting me know your favorite part of the story—nothing fancy required, even a sentence or two would be wonderful—I would be deeply grateful.

About the Author

Lili Valente has slept under the stars in Greece, eaten dinner at midnight with French men who couldn't be trusted to keep their mouths on their food, and walked alone through Munich's red light district after dark and lived to tell the tale.

These days you can find her writing in a tent beside the sea, drinking coconut water and thinking delightfully dirty thoughts.

Lili loves to hear from her readers. You can reach her via email at
lili.valente.romance@gmail.com
or like her page on Facebook
https://www.facebook.com/AuthorLiliValente

You can also visit her website:
http://www.lilivalente.com/

Also By Lili Valente

Bad Motherpuckers Books:
Hot as Puck
Sexy Motherpucker
Puck Aholic

Sexy Flirty Dirty Series:
Magnificent Bastard
Spectacular Rascal
Incredible You

The Under His Command Series:
Controlling Her Pleasure
Commanding Her Trust
Claiming Her Heart

The Bought by the Billionaire Series:
Dark Domination
Deep Domination
Desperate Domination
Divine Domination

The Kidnapped by the Billionaire Series:
Dirty Twisted Love
Filthy Wicked Love
Crazy Beautiful Love
One More Shameless Night

The Bedding the Bad Boy Series:
The Bad Boy's Temptation
The Bad Boy's Seduction
The Bad Boy's Redemption

Sneak Peek of Puck Aholic

CHAPTER ONE

Tanner AKA Nowicki

Tonight, I helped a friend propose to the woman he loves. I made two people who are perfect for each other very happy, solidified a bond with a teammate I admire, and got to watch the sunset from the deck of a multimillion-dollar beachside mansion where I'll be spending the night with a group of good friends and their families.

I finally made the list. I'm a "cool kid."

As a rookie, there was a time—like two months ago—when I didn't get invited to the smaller, veteran parties, the private gatherings of the players who know they've got a home in Portland as long as they stay fast enough and refrain from getting their heads slammed into the glass too often. Concussions take out a lot of good players before their time.

And then there are guys like me, whose

brains are hardwired wrong from the get-go. My contract was renewed for next year, but if I don't keep my focus laser-sharp, I might not be a Badger for long.

It would be best if I don't get attached. Don't get in too deep. Don't allow myself to wish I wasn't at this party alone.

I don't have time for a girlfriend, and I'm in no place to make a long-term commitment.

But as I watch my teammates pair off with their significant others—wandering down to the darkened beach or up to their rooms—I can't help feeling low.

And cranky.

And a little jealous.

Fine, a lot jealous. Until this year, I haven't spent much time alone. I've always had a girlfriend or a steady date on the verge of becoming a girlfriend. I like women, have always gotten along well with the better-smelling sex, and enjoy spending time with humans who aren't afraid to talk about things other than sports or work, which happen to be the same in my world, further reducing the opportunities for conversational variety.

And then there's sex…

I sigh heavily as I plod down the stairs toward the beach, my flask of whiskey in hand.

God, I fucking miss fucking. I miss it so much I'm starting to wonder if there's something wrong with me.

Surely even the most testosterone-fueled meatheads don't think about sex as much as I think about sex. And the only thing that keeps me from dwelling on how long it's been since I had a woman in my bed—seven months, three days, and a handful of hours—is killing myself on the ice at practice and pushing myself to the limit during every game.

But now I have a four-week hiatus until practices officially start again and nothing but my morning workouts to keep my thoughts out of the gutter.

Summer hookup, man.

There's nothing wrong with something temporary as long as you're honest with the girl before you get in too deep.

I tip back my flask, sending more Johnny Walker Blue flowing into my mouth, so smoky and smooth there isn't a hint of burning when I swallow.

A summer hookup won't work. I know myself better than that. If I find a girl I like enough to want to fuck her, I'm going to want to keep fucking her and caring about her and moving forward until something eventually gets in the way. And if that something is me needing to end things because I can't keep my head in the game or I get transferred to an armpit team in Arizona, I'll feel like an asshole.

"Alone," I mutter, lifting my flask to the black ocean waves crashing against the sand as I stop at the darkest, loneliest corner of the beach. The place where I clearly belong. "Better to go it alone."

The words have barely passed my lips when something warm and smelling pleasantly of campfire with a hint of musk collides with my backside, sending me stumbling forward a few unsteady steps.

"Oh my God, I'm sorry!" A female giggle follows the apology and a slim hand grips my arm. "Are you okay? Did I hurt you?" She giggles again, as if the idea of injuring strangers amuses her.

I smile, figuring it's probably time to lay off the whiskey if a collision with a kid half my size has me off balance. I can't see the girl's face well in the dim light from the sliver of moon, but she's tiny, probably no more than sixteen or seventeen. "No, I'm fine. But should you be down here by yourself?"

"Should *you* be down here by yourself?" She brings a cigarette to her lips and inhales, making the tip flare. "I hear this beach has killer mermaids." She giggles again as she exhales, sending that musky, almost skunky smell drifting through the air again, making me realize that's no cigarette.

"Killer mermaids?" I ask, deciding to play along. "Is that right?"

She nods. "Killer, carnivorous mermaids. And they like guys like you most of all." She grips my arm again, giving my bicep a squeeze. "Mmm, yes, nice juicy muscles. So dee-lish-usssss…"

I flex beneath her touch because I am a man and it's hardwired into my DNA to flex like a cheesy bastard when my muscles are fondled, even if the person feeling me up is a wasted teenager.

"Nice," she says, clucking her tongue as she squeezes my other arm. "Too bad you're going to be mermaid-bait pretty soon."

"So it's too late, you think? To make a run for safety?"

She nods with a heavy sigh. "Yes, sadly, it's too late. They'll be here any second. Can't you hear them? Laughing in the waves?"

We both go silent for a moment, listening, before my wasted companion starts giggling again. "Sorry," she says, "That was me. Don't be afraid. That was me laughing."

"Yeah, I could tell." I arch an amused brow. "Maybe you should put that out, and save the rest for later?"

"I'm sorry. Where are my manners?" She moves the blunt between us. "You want some? It's good. Smooth, not too heavy. Takes the edge off a shit start to the weekend."

"No thanks, I don't smoke," I say, beginning to think I've misjudged her age.

Yes, she's petite, but the world-weary note in her voice is pure disillusioned grownup. "I'm Tanner, by the way."

"Hey, Tanner." She accepts the hand I hold out, shaking it firmly. "You here for the party? Back there?"

"Yeah. You?" I wonder if she's someone's girlfriend and realize I don't like how that wondering makes me feel. I haven't even seen this woman—or girl, I'm still not sure—clearly, and I'm already starting to develop a crush.

Fuck, I need to get laid. Or stop drinking whiskey. Or both.

"Nah." She shakes her head, making her ponytail—blonde, I think, or light brown, and a little curly—swish. "Just here to help with a family thing. My brother's girlfriend proposed to him tonight and needed me to help facilitate the fucking romance."

I grunt. "That's crazy. My friend proposed to his girlfriend tonight, too. I was in charge of guarding the stairwell to make sure no one disturbed them until she said yes."

"And did she?"

"Yeah. How about your brother?"

She makes an exasperated growling sound. "Yes. And it was ridiculously romantic, and they cried because they're so happy and in love." She takes another pull on her joint, holding the smoke in as she adds, "If I didn't love them so much, I would have vomited. I'm so over happy couples right now. They're so fucking gross."

I grin. "They are kind of gross."

"Totally gross." She nudges me with her elbow. "So I guess you aren't living happily ever after?"

"Not currently, how about you?"

She snorts. "No. Not now, not ever. Ten years of trying, and all I've got to show for it is a handful of Mr. Wrongs and a Mr. Right I broke up with because I dated him too soon after Mr. Super Duper Wrong and was too stupid to see that I was running away from the best thing that had ever happened to me. And now he's engaged, too, and life is dumb, and I'm done with relationships. I'm probably going to move to Tibet and become a monk."

"Aren't monks men?"

"Yeah." She shrugs as she drops the nub her joint has become to the ground and toes sand over it. "I'll have to pretend to be a guy, I guess. But how hard can that be? Just cut my hair, drop my voice, walk funny, and check to make sure my dick is still there a lot. Easy."

I tilt my head, studying her face, which I'm finally able to see better now that the clouds covering the moon have been swept away by the wind. She's pretty. Very pretty. With full lips that dominate her pixie face and expressive eyebrows that make squiggles above her eyes as she asks, "What?"

"Nothing. I just think you might be too pretty to pull off pretending to be a guy. Sorry."

"You should be sorry. I hate it when sexy men with nice muscles tell me I'm pretty." She grins up at me as she places a hand on my chest and leans in to add in a confidential whisper, "Just in case you're wondering, I'm hitting on you, and I think we should make out on the sand. What do you think?"

I blink, surprised, but not at all opposed to the idea, assuming…

"How old are you?" I step closer. If she's been dating for ten years, she's got to be at least in her early twenties, but it's better safe than sorry.

"Older than you are, Muscle Boy. Does that matter?"

"I'm twenty-four," I say, seriously doubting her claim. She looks twenty-one, maybe twenty-two, tops.

"Twenty-seven." Her arms go around my neck, and her breasts press against my chest, proving she's curvier than I thought, too. "Is that enough getting to know each other? Can we casually make out now?"

My lips part, but before I can speak, she's pushed up on tiptoe and pressed her lips to mine. And I don't know if it's the whiskey, or the dark beach and the crash of the waves, or the strange, yet oddly comforting conversation—I'm not the only one who's alone and not too pleased about it—but the kiss is…incredible.

She tastes like woodsy, slightly funky smoke, but sweet, too. A perfect mixture of bad influence and warm, sexy woman. And as we tumble to the sand, I find myself feeling happier than I have in a damned long time.

We kiss for what seems like hours, like teenagers—hot, hungry, hands roaming, but never slipping under clothes—before she whispers against my lips, "Thank you. I needed to touch someone tonight."

"You're welcome," I say, my next words slipping out before I can think better of them. "You can sleep over if you want. I'm staying at the house back there. King bed, plenty of room, no pressure to take things any further."

"Oh, Muscle Boy…" She sighs as her hand skims down my stomach to hover close to where my canvas shorts are strained at the front. Her fingers tease back and forth between my skin and the button holding the fabric closed, making the hard-on situation even more…pressing. "If I went back to your room, I would want a lot more than kissing."

"That's fine, too." All my promises not to start something this summer are forgotten as I imagine how insanely good it's going to feel to make my beach pixie come and finally break my seven-month dry spell.

"No, it's not." She pulls away, out of my arms, moving to sit beside me on the sand. "I have to go home."

"I can call a car for you in the morning," I say. "First thing."

She shakes her head. "Can't. I'm moving tomorrow, and I still have to pack. My friend is coming to pick me up in half an hour. I promised her I would be out by noon. I think she's sick of having my life exploded all over her living room."

I nod, crestfallen, but trying not to show it. It's pretty clear she's not interested in more than casual beach kisses and an easy "see ya later." But I can't seem to stop myself from saying, "What about tomorrow night? Can I take you to dinner? Maybe bowling or something?"

She grins, giggling again as she leans in, resting her head on my shoulder. "Oh, you're sweet. Very, very sweet." She kisses my arm, right where my T-shirt ends. "But I'm not that kind of girl anymore, Muscle Boy. You keep looking. Find yourself someone sweet and new who isn't cursed with the worst love-life luck on the planet."

I start to protest—to tell her I'm not afraid of bad luck—but before I can speak, her lips are on mine. She kisses me again, until I'm even harder, aching, dying to roll her beneath me in the sand and make her feel so good she'll change her mind about staying with me tonight and dinner tomorrow.

But when I move to guide her on top of me, she pulls away, standing up and backing across the sand so fast she's already disappearing into the darkness when she says, "Good luck, Tanner. Thank you again."

Then she's gone, and I'm alone.

And suddenly the thought of waking up tomorrow surrounded by people in love is intolerable. With another pull on my flask, I head up the beach and march straight to my room, throwing my shit into my bag as I call for a car. I rode here with Saunders and his girlfriend, but I'm sure they won't mind making the return trip alone.

Hell, they'll prefer it, no doubt.

No fucking doubt…

And there is no doubt in my mind that I'm

never going to see my sexy beach pixie again. By the time I tumble into my bed at home an hour later, she's already becoming something distant, a memory touched by magic. The entire encounter was too strange to be real. Maybe she was one of those killer mermaids she warned me about, come onto the beach to hunt for men stupid enough to wander too close to the waves.

For all I know, I could have barely escaped with my life.

The thought is ridiculous, childish even, but it makes the rejection sting less, and by the time I wake up the next morning I've all but forgotten about the girl I kissed last night.

When Brendan, my team captain calls, telling me his little sister's new living situation fell through, and asking if I'm still looking for a roommate, I don't for a single second consider the chance that I might have met his sister before. That I might have kissed her, rocked against her through our clothes, wanted to make love to her more than I've wanted anything in a very, very long time.

I'm clueless and say yes without a second

thought, not realizing what a serious fucking mistake I've made until I answer the front door an hour later to find Beach Pixie standing on my doorstep, wearing cut-offs, a tank top so thin it should be illegal, and a shocked expression that matches my own.

Puck Aholic is coming
your way Summer 2017!

Printed in Great Britain
by Amazon